DEMAIN PUB

CW00406654

Short Sharp Shocks!

Murder! Mystery! Mayhem!

Beats! Ballads! Blank Verse!

Book 1: Echoes From An Expired Earth – Allen Ashley
Book 2: Grave Goods – Cardinal Cox
Book 3: From Long Ago – Paul Woodward
Book 4: Laws Of Discord – William Clunie
Book 5: Fanged Dandelion – Eric LaRocca

Weird! Wonderful! Other Worlds

Book 1: The Raven King – Liz Tuckwell
Book 2: The Wired City – Yolanda Sfetsos

Horror Novels & Novellas

House Of Wrax – Raven Dane
A Quiet Apocalypse – Dave Jeffery
Cathedral (A Quiet Apocalypse Book 2) – Dave Jeffery
And Blood Did Fall – Chad A. Clark
The Underclass – Dan Weatherer
Cheslyn Myre – Dan Weatherer
Greenbeard – John Travis
The Raven Kiing – Kevin M. Folliard
Little Bird – TR Hitchman
Society Place – Andrew David Barker

General Fiction

Joe – Terry Grimwood
Finding Jericho – Dave Jeffery

Science Fiction Collections

Vistas – Chris Kelso

Horror Fiction Collections

Distant Frequencies – Frank Duffy
Where We Live – Tim Cooke
Night Voices – Paul Edwards & Frank Duffy

Anthologies

The Darkest Battlefield – Tales Of WW1/Horror

SOCIETY PLACE

BY
ANDREW DAVID BARKER

Andrew David Barker

Nov, 2021

For further information, please visit:
WEB: www.demainpublishing.com
TWITTER: @DemainPubUk
FACEBOOK: Demain Publishing
INSTAGRAM: demainpublishing

For my mother, Linda

CONTENTS

"Some are born to sweet delight, some are born to endless night." - William Blake

A house has walls. Bricks and mortar. They are built by hand, from the ground up. From foundations dug deep into earth.

Windows let the light in. Roof trusses rest above us. Slates darken in the rain.

Inside, bathrooms are fitted. Electricity is wired down walls and beneath floorboards. Beds are made. Ovens fill kitchens with aromas. Babies are born.

People grow. They weather storms, and laugh with joy, and cry into the night. There are Christmases, and summers, and autumn leaves that pile up in gardens. Doorsteps are swept. Curtains are drawn. People move in, people move away. Some feel trapped, others feel sanctuary.

They wallpaper and paint, and fix doors and replace windows. They strip away the lingering scent of others and turn the bricks and mortar into a home and the cycle goes on.

People live. People die. They love, they despair. Sometimes bad things happen. Sometimes there is beautiful tenderness. Every aspect of the human condition plays out. We bleed into the walls.

And houses can stand for generations. Some cross into new centuries. Sometimes they are a home, other times nothing but a shell.

Yes, houses have walls. And they soak all of us up.

Every last drop.

PART ONE
1976

CHAPTER ONE

Heather Lowes picked the keys up from the Estate Agents on a blazing August morning and walked through the town, heading for Society Place. On the way she took note of street names and shops, acquainting herself with the landscape of her new life. She stopped off at a store on Normanton Road called Presto's and bought a few cleaning products, a box of tea bags, a bottle of milk, and a few other odds and sods, then continued on her way to the new house.

Her brother was set to arrive later that day in his Bedford van, loaded up with Heather's entire world—a bed, a tatty two-piece sofa, television set, a black bin bag of clothes, a few pots and pans, and general knick-knacks—but first she planned to get to the house, give it a good airing and a clean-up, and get to know the place.

Laden with shopping bags, she traipsed up Silver Hill Road, which was surprisingly steep, and sweaty and irritated, Heather reached the top and turned onto Society Place.

She thought the name grand and sophisticated. The reality however was a row of unremarkable pre-war terrace houses, drab and decidedly English. On the other side of the road was a high brick wall, behind which lay the backyards of houses further up the rise.

There were rubbish bags piled up in the street, a guy with a motorbike in pieces out on the pavement (she had to navigate herself around this), kids kicking a ball about in the middle of the road, and Led Zeppelin blasting from one particular house, and 10CC from another. House fronts were flat, doors stepping straight out onto the pavement. Many of these doors were left open. There were no front gardens, and no trees. No green of any kind in fact, just bricks and mortar, pavement and road. The sky a strip of brilliant blue between the rooftops.

Heather walked the length of the street and came to stand outside number 2, her new home. She stood for a moment, taking in the tatty windows and paint-peeled door. The net-curtains twitched in the house next door.

One of the kids came running by. He frowned at Heather, looking her up and down, then picked up his ball and walked over.

"You going in that house, Miss?"

He was scrawny, grubby, with an unfortunate cleft lip that made him look a little aggressive. Heather judged he was about eight or nine years old.

"Yes, I am," she said.

He seemed surprised by this. "You gonna live there?"

She glanced at the house. "As a matter of fact, I am."

"No one's lived in that house for years."

"Well, I'm going to live there now. My name's Heather."

"My name's Rafferty, but everybody calls me Raff."

"Hello, Raff."

One of the other kids down the street called to him. "Come on, Raff, giz the ball."

Raff shouted back, "In a sec," then turned his attention back to Heather. "You gonna live there on your own?"

It seemed to Heather he said this with genuine concern, which she found a little disconcerting.

"Yes, Raff, I am."

"You not married?"

Heather fought against a sudden wave of tears. The other boys, their patience at an end, gave a unified cry for the ball. Raff took note of their tone and began backing away from Heather.

"I live at number 9, Miss, with my mum and dad."

"I'll be sure to come and introduce myself once I'm settled in, Raff."

He smiled at this then ran off down the street, kicking the ball back to his mates. Heather turned back to the house. She wiped her eyes with the back of her hand and composed herself. Next door's curtains twitched again.

Heather collected up her shopping and approached the front door. She slid the key in and turned. It was a little stiff and took a few attempts before the lock would give. Once open however, she shoved the door inwards against the pile of letters on the carpet and stood out on the street peering into the dusty dark of the front room. She could smell the musty air inside.

Then, with one glance back down the street, she crossed the threshold into her new home: Number 2, Society Place, Normanton, Derby.

***

The first thing she did was go room to room, opening all curtains and windows. She also opened the back door. The house was a small two-up, two-down: front room and kitchen downstairs, with two bedrooms upstairs. The back bedroom had a partitioned sink and bath, but bizarrely no toilet—the toilet was outside. It did, however, have a cellar, which Heather had yet to see, having not ventured down there on her one and only viewing of the property back in spring, back when Tony had still been alive.

In the kitchen, Heather filled the sink with cold water and placed the milk in it then she took a moment to take in her new surroundings. The house was filthy and it smelled stale and earthy. She sighed at the amount of work to be done.

On Heather and Tony's viewing back in April, the estate agent had let slip that no one had lived in the house since 1971. When asked as to why the place had been empty for five years, the estate agent, a rather stern, slender woman with Farrah Fawcett hair, could not (or would not) elaborate.

Heather had been wholly unimpressed on that first viewing, but Tony had been of the mind that, with a little care and attention, the house could be a good starter home for them. "The price is really good," he'd argued, and to this Heather had to agree. Everything else they'd viewed had been well out of their price range. 2, Society Place, on the other hand, was on the market for £1,500, and in no chain. After a £150 deposit (which Tony's parents had offered to loan them), the mortgage payments would be £6 a week. Just about manageable. Tony also said that the back bedroom would make a good nursery. She remembered looking up at him when he'd said this and seeing a big, stupid grin on his face. That had been the clincher.

They put an offer in on the house and the William Plant Estate Agents rang later that day to say that the house was theirs. Heather felt pure bliss as they danced around Tony's parent's house (where they'd been living since getting married in February), and they went out that night and got a little drunk and came back and made love in the kitchen while Tony's folks slept upstairs. Afterwards, as she lay by her husband in bed, Heather knew she had become pregnant.

***

Tony died in a car crash two weeks later.

***

She began in the kitchen, scrubbing out cupboards and worktops, bleaching the sink, and taking a wire-brush to the gas cooker. With the back door open she could hear the kids out on the street and the distant sound of an ice cream van's melodic chimes. The day was nothing short of a scorcher, well into the high 80s at least, and Heather drank straight from the tap several times, splashing her face and hair in an effort to cool down. The heat was oppressive and unrelenting. It had been all summer.

After sweeping the kitchen floor, she went and sat on the back door step. The yard was small, concreted, with a fence on one side and a high wall on the other. It felt very enclosed. The privy outhouse was a narrow brick building at the end of the yard. It looked in complete disrepair; several slates were missing from its roof and the door was hanging on for dear life by one hinge and a couple of loose screws. She dreaded to think what it looked like inside. She only hoped the toilet itself worked.

There was a crooked back gate, which led out into a jitty, and a pile of old bricks and rubble up against the outhouse. No greenery whatsoever. Heather wondered if she'd made a huge mistake in taking the house on, but then, what choice did she have? She was a twenty-four year old pregnant widow with little money and nowhere else to go. There really hadn't been many options. She'd far outstayed her welcome at Tom and Jean's house, the situation becoming toxic after Tony's death. Her own mum and dad were also in the ground, so that just left her brother, Mike, but he lived in a bedsit with his revolving girlfriends, a mountain of amplifiers and guitars, and a perpetual haze of hashish. It'd been Society Place or nowhere. Still, if truth be known, she had wanted the house. It had been the place she and Tony had chosen to live, and she felt she needed to honour that decision.

His face was so clear and real to her still—*so alive*, she thought. She had fought hard not think of him all morning, but now his image, his *presence*, filled her up and she broke down. Since Tony's funeral, the waves of grief were often sudden and all-consuming. The tears pulled her inwards, down into the dark. The bright day floated away. The absence of him was like a great black hole in her very being. She felt as if she were now half a person; a vessel where once a whole, real, living girl used to be.

Distantly, she felt something on her wrist. Through blurry eyes she saw it was a ladybird. She turned her hand over and found another in her palm. There was a third moving down her other arm. She shook them off and put her hands to her face.

How long she'd been sat crying on the back step for, she had no idea, but she was pulled back up into the light by a banging on the front door. She could hear her brother calling her name. He sounded very, very far away.

***

"Bleeding hell, Heather, I've been knocking for ages."

Mike was stood with an album cover attitude, his usual stance, shirt unbuttoned down to the breastbone, wearing tight bell-bottoms and a pair of bright blue brothel creepers. They looked brand new. He had a thick beard, dark eyes, a black nest of curly hair—*à la* Syd Barrett or Marc Bolan—and the obligatory fag was hanging out of his mouth. As their mother used to say, he was a legend in his own lunchtime.

"Sorry, Mike," said Heather, "I was just...busy in the kitchen."

Mike noticed that she had been crying and softened, "It's okay, Poppy."

Poppy was a childhood nickname, a pet name originated by their father and adopted in later life by Mike. He only called her it very rarely but when he did it always moved her. She bit back further tears and he stepped inside, wrapping his arms around her. She nestled into his shirt and he kissed the top of her head. He smelled of Brut.

"Come on then, sis," he said, "You gonna show me 'round this dump or what?"

She smiled into his shirt.

***

Heather took her brother on a tour of the house. It didn't take very long. In the back bedroom Mike peered out of the window, down into the yard, and across the other gardens. The backs of houses on Silver Hill Road and Corporation Street were also visible from the window. There was a single tall tree stood within this network of gardens, vast and ancient. A dog was barking from a kennel several doors down.

"That sun is beating like a bastard," said Mike, turning from the window.

"What do you think to the house?"

"Yeah," he said with very little conviction.

"You think I've made a mistake, don't you?"

"No, Heather, I don't think that. It's just…"

"Just what?"

"There's a lot of work to do here."

"I know."

"You sure you're gonna be able to handle it? On your own, I mean…"

"I'll be fine, Michael. Working on the house will take my mind off things."

She could see he wasn't very convinced. He took a look in the partitioned bathroom.

"Where's the toilet?" he asked.

"Outside."

"Oh, Heather. I know its scorching hot now but what about come winter when the baby's due?" The pity in his voice was sickening.

"I'll manage."

"You're gonna need all amenities inside, Heather, and—"

"I will manage."

He knew by her tone to drop it. A moment passed between them then Mike rubbed his hands together and said, "Right, all your junk ain't gonna get in here by itself is it?"

***

Tony died on a dull, overcast May afternoon. Heather had been to the market with Tony's mother, Jean, to pick up that night's dinner. Jean was of a generation of women who went shopping every day, buying only the evening meal and, if needed, stocking up on tins for the pantry (two of everything was required at all times). Only on Saturdays did Jean buy for two days: Saturday night's meal, usually something with chips, and the Sunday roast. That was known as 'the big shop'.

It had started to drizzle by the time they got back to the house. Jean put the shopping away then the kettle went straight on. The biscuit tin was always full and always accompanied by a pot of tea. Heather liked the fig rolls best. They sat at the kitchen table and chit-chatted. Jean did most of the talking, running through such topics as the weather, James Callaghan, Tom's arthritis, and the best way to make a beef stew, all, seemingly, without coming up for air. Heather picked out the fig rolls and the odd chocolate Bourbon, half listening, and thought about Tony.

He had gone to work that morning in a dark mood. He'd seemed tired and fraught. Heather had told him the night before that she couldn't wait to move into the house on Society Place; there they could properly begin their lives together as man and wife. Tom and Jean had been very kind and accommodating to the newlyweds but it had been far from easy. They had no real privacy and Heather often felt ill at ease. If Tony and Heather tried to discuss something between themselves, Jean would always cut in and want to know what they were talking about. She didn't mean any harm, it just seemed to be her nature. She liked to natter, or as Tom subtly put it, "That woman can rattle for England."

Tom was a hard man to read. He was barrel-chested, said very little, and seemed to just want to be left alone to watch his beloved westerns, or, for variation, a war film. Trying to have a conversation with him was like pulling teeth, even for Tony. He was the mirror opposite to his wife when it came to engaging with other people. He'd been a bricklayer by trade, but back problems and arthritis took him out of that game. He drank down the Legion every afternoon and expected his dinner on the table when he got home, and it always was on the table, without fail. Heather had never seen Tom and Jean share any intimacy, and often watched in amusement, and a little sadness, when Jean would sit and talk at him while he'd sit glum and unresponsive in front of John Wayne or Audie Murphy.

Tom was out at the Legion on that rainy May afternoon. Jean had just started to peel the spuds for dinner when there was a knock at the door. Heather was upstairs folding some clothes and listened as Jean answered the door. She heard muffled voices and then Jean cried out. Heather rushed downstairs to find Jean sitting on the front mat crying and two police officers stood in the doorway. One of the officers—older and more authoritative looking than the other—asked Heather if she was the wife of Anthony Lowes. She nodded and then the policeman told her that her husband of four months was dead, killed in a head-on collision involving three other cars on a B road in Duffield. Two other people had also been killed.

Heather sat on the stairs. She looked at the carpet in the hall and thought how tatty and ugly it was. She noticed that her hands were shaking very badly. She looked at Jean, wailing in a crumpled heap on her horrible carpet. She looked at the policemen and wondered how many times they'd had to deliver news of this kind. She thought about the life she'd had when she was upstairs folding clothes, how it'd been heading in a certain direction, and how, now downstairs, that life had been irrevocably changed—obliterated, in point of fact—in the space of a few seconds.

Tony Lowes had been twenty-four years old. He never knew of the baby growing inside his wife. She herself wouldn't learn she was pregnant until the week after the funeral, although she had suspected she was. When her doctor confirmed it, she was five weeks gone and hearing the words, "Congratulations, you're pregnant!" was the single most joyous and painful thing she had ever heard in her life.

***

Michael carried Heather's belongings into the house. Rafferty hung around Mike's Bedford van, jabbering away, and even helped carry a few things inside. It didn't take long to get everything in. Mike set up Heather's bed in the front bedroom, and then got busy with the television downstairs. Heather sorted through her clothes and put covers on the bed.

Once the television was set up, Mike said he had to rush off. He had a gig that night with his band, Candlestick Park, and had to go home and load up all the gear in the van. He asked Heather if she'd like to come.

"Where you playing?" she asked.

"A Working Man's up in Belper."

"Think I'll give this one a miss, Mike. Sorry."

"No bother," he said then looked at her. "You gonna to be alright?"

She nodded but didn't say anything.

"Well," he said, "I better go."

"Okay."

He kissed her forehead.

She looked up at him. "Thank you, Mike."

"It's fine, Poppy. You get settled in. Everything's going to be alright."

He walked out of the kitchen, through the front room, and out into the street. He closed the door behind him.

Heather leaned against the sink, looked around, and held her belly.

CHAPTER TWO

Heather set the radio up in the kitchen. She tuned it in to Radio Caroline and found Wings singing *Silly Love Songs*. She moved from room to room, getting a sense of the house. She couldn't quite believe this was now her home, and seeing her meagre belongings in this new environment was decidedly odd; her girlhood bed strangest of all in the otherwise bare front bedroom.

The walls were covered in flowery-patterned wallpaper throughout, all browns and yellows, and the carpet was a deep burgundy, matted and threadbare. Nothing matched. She wondered if the house had seen a lick of paint or a new roll of wallpaper since the war, and decided that it almost certainly had not. The kitchen was as basic as basic got; the units were falling to bits, the cooker a relic, and there were cracked tiles around the sink—some had dropped out entirely. Around the rest of the house there were curtain rails hanging out of walls, missing pieces of skirting-board, rotten doorframes, and a cellar so full of junk it was impassable.

She sat on the back step again, listening to the radio and wondered where to begin. She had no idea how to start this new life.

***

Tom and Jean nipped 'round in the afternoon to drop off a vacuum cleaner—a housewarming gift—and to have a nose around (Jean zipped from room to room like a terrier). They didn't stay long.

Once they left it occurred to Heather that neither one of them had asked how she was. She may have been carrying their grandchild, but without Tony, Heather wondered if she meant anything at all to her in-laws. She knew she wouldn't see much of them now, if at all. Still, they'd bought her a vacuum, and as there was at least five years worth of dirt upon the carpets, it was a much needed, and much appreciated, present. She set to work right away.

She began in the front room, hoovering around the back of her television, then moving the sofa from one position to another, making sure she got every inch of the carpet. That done, she carried the vacuum through the kitchen and set to work on the stairs. It was cumbersome and tiresome work. The stairs were narrow and walled in on either side. The light at the top of the stairs was dim and it took a long while for her eyes to adjust after being in the brightness of the day. The vacuum sounded very loud in the narrow stairway.

Once she reached the top of the stairs, she went into her bedroom and hoovered up in there. She shoved the head of the vacuum as far under her bed as she could then lifted the entire contraption and hoovered up around the window sill. She looked down into the street and saw the boy, Rafferty, still kicking his ball about. He appeared to be alone.

He caught sight of her and smiled and waved. Heather put the vacuum down and waved back. Then something odd happened. Rafferty's expression changed in an instant, his smile falling away. Heather frowned. He looked troubled, unnerved even. Also, he no longer seemed to be looking directly at her, but past her, as if at something else in the room. Heather felt the hairs on her neck bristle and she turned and looked around. The room was empty. She laughed then looked back down at Rafferty but he was gone, running off down the street. She pressed her face against the glass and caught sight of him disappearing into his house.

He left his ball at the kerb.

She continued to hoover up but couldn't shake the image of the little boy's face. He'd looked genuinely scared, she thought on reflection.

She let the vacuum run, but didn't push it around. She stood and looked around the room. She'd left the door ajar, the top of the stairs beyond. She reached down and clicked the vacuum off. It whirred down. The house was still, the tinny sound of the radio playing downstairs. A dog was barking somewhere far off.

She shook her head, muttering, "What am I doing?"

She turned the vacuum back on and pushed Rafferty's little face out of her mind. It'd more than likely been a nine-year-old's idea of a joke anyway. Nothing more, she told herself.

There were a lot of dark stains on the bedroom carpet that would require some industrial strength cleaner and a lot of scrubbing. A job for another day. She finished up and then moved into the back bedroom. She didn't look down into the stairway as she crossed it.

***

The carpet in the back bedroom was in an even worse state. She took a breather and looked out across the gardens. Her t-shirt clung to her back. She opened the partitioned door and weighed up how much scrubbing she was going to have to do before she could get in the bath. To dip in a tub of cold water would have been glorious but she had too much to do, and besides, she was going to have to scrub and bleach that thing before she put any part of her body in it. She sighed then returned to the window. The tree was in full bloom, reaching over several gardens. Heather thought it to be an ash tree, although she wasn't a hundred percent. The leaves were a rich green, and its trunk, thick and deeply gnarled. The tree drew the eye.

She made a plan: she'd finish the hoovering, clean the bath and sink, then have a break and get something to eat. The thought of food spurred her on and she went back to vacuum. Before turning it on however she felt compelled to look up. As before, the bedroom door was half open, giving only a glimpse of the dim stairway.

The sensation of somebody being out there, on the stairs, came on very strong.

Heather stared at the door for a long time. Nothing moved. She had to force her eyes away. She looked at her arms and saw they were covered in goose pimples. She also felt them down her legs. She walked over and grabbed the door handle, then stood motionless, listening hard. The house seemed to oblige with a few creaks and groans. She could hear the faint strains of *The Jean Genie* coming from the radio down in the kitchen. From outside came sounds of the summer, reassuring in its melody of squealing kids and balls thumping against walls. She tried to block all that out and listened for any sound coming directly from the stairway. All was silent, yet something still didn't feel right. She pictured a man stood at the top of the stairs, his face pressed up against the other side of the door. A shot ran down her spine at this image and she shivered. Then, almost involuntary, she laughed again.

"This is ridiculous," she said, and shut the door, hard.

She finished hoovering up, singing loudly to herself.

***

She not only scrubbed out the bath but also tackled the outside toilet. She ran the vacuum lead from the kitchen and dragged the contraption down the yard and hoovered out all the dirt and cobwebs. The lead only just reached. She turned the radio up and sang along while she worked. The privy wasn't quite as bad as she'd fear, and after half an hour's work, she'd got it looking almost presentable. She used the toilet once her work was done.

She worked through lunch and deep into the afternoon. She just got on and completely forgot about food. At five o'clock she washed her hands and face in the kitchen sink and stood looking at her house. Thin Lizzy were on the radio doing *The Boys Are Back in Town*. Tony had liked Thin Lizzy and she found herself humming along to it. The hazy late afternoon light filled the world with promise. She felt hopeful for the first time in weeks and weeks and weeks.

She decided to go out and grab some food from somewhere. She went up to her bedroom, rifled through her bag of clothes and found a fresh t-shirt to wear. Downstairs, she grabbed her keys and her handbag and then stepped out onto Society Place.

***

All the local kids must have gone in for their tea because Society Place and the surrounding streets were now deserted. She headed for the neighbouring Corporation Street and walked further up the hill. The light was golden and Heather wished the world could always look this way: sun-kissed and elegant.

A little way up the rise she passed a school. It looked harsh, with its red-bricked, flat frontage, and rows of large windows. It struck Heather that it looked more like a Victorian workhouse than a school. Its entrance lay to side of the building, up a small flight of steps. She read the sign above the gate: Saint Chad's Church of England Nursery and Infant School. As it was August, the place was all shut up and perhaps because of this, it felt quite an imposing, even oppressive, place.

She passed this Dickensian structure and headed to the top of the rise. Here she found a main road and a corner shop: A. Singh's Grocers, News & Convenience Store. Handy, she thought. She stood on the kerb, waited for several cars to pass, then crossed the road and entered the shop.

A Punjabi man was stood behind the counter. He gave her a smile and a warm, "Hello," as she came in. She returned this. He was a large man; thick eyebrows, long, full beard, wearing a striking blue turban and a brown salwar. He had a kindly face and he watched her as she navigated the narrow aisles. She took a basket and picked up bread, loo rolls, and some cheese—all life's essentials. She figured she'd do a 'big shop'—as Jean would call it—tomorrow. For now, just a few bits would do.

The shopkeeper gave her a huge grin and went through the basket pricing up the items. He did this by memory.

"I've not seen you in here before," he said. He spoke fast and his accent was thick so Heather didn't quite catch what he'd said at first.

"You new 'round here?" he added.

"I am," she said, "I've just moved in. Today, in fact."

"Oh, good, good."

"Yes, it's been a bit manic."

"Moving house is always a pain in the bum."

Heather laughed. There was an openness to this man that put her at ease.

"I've moved down on Society Place."

"Ah, so you're our new local girl. Well, welcome to your new local shop. Make sure you come here for all your needs. My name is Amar, but you can call me Mr Singh." She laughed. He continued. "I will also respond to Your Lordship. Or, if you just want to keep it simple, just plain old Sir. I'm easy."

This really made Heather giggle.

He totalled everything up on his till. "Three forty nine please, Miss…"

"Oh, sorry, my name is Heather. Heather Lowes." She got her purse out.

"Well Heather Lowes, pleased to make your acquaintance."

He offered his hand and they shook.

Heather paid him with a fiver. He counted the change out into her palm. She put the money back in her purse and smiled at him.

"Well Mr Singh, Your Lordship, Sir! I'll bid you good day."

"Very good, Heather Lowes," he said, grinning a mouthful of teeth.

***

She stood outside the shop and looked down the rise. From this vantage point Heather had a fine view of her new world. The sun was low in the sky and rooftops shimmered and the air hummed and it all felt resplendent. In that moment, she felt good about what she'd taken on. A positive first step on the road to a new life.

She was about to cross over when she spied a fish and chip shop a hundred or so yards down from where she stood. She walked to it and ordered herself a small cod, chips, and a fritter. The young girl working in there wasn't particularly friendly. Heather had the food wrapped up so she could take it home and eat it. She hadn't realised how hungry she was until she smelt those fish and chips.

She walked back down the rise with all her shopping, looking forward to eating, taking a long bath, and simply enjoying time to herself, something she hadn't been able to do for a long, long time.

***

When she got in, Heather spread butter on some bread, plated up the fish, chips and fritter, then went through to the front room. She turned the TV on, cursed when she realised Michael hadn't tuned it in, and spent five minutes fiddling about with the controls. She finally got BBC1 and a wavy BBC2, but couldn't get ITV for the life of her, so she had to settle with just the two channels. She watched the cricket on BBC2 and ate her dinner. It felt very good to get some food inside her.

Her plate demolished, she drifted off to sleep on the sofa. She had no idea how long she was out for but when she woke the room was a lot darker. The cricket had finished and there were some ballet dancers on. She looked at her watch: it was coming on for half past eight. She got up and turned over to BBC1 and watched *Seaside Special*, a variety show hosted by Larry Grayson, this week featuring Roy

Hudd and The Wurzels. It was terrible, but she was too tired to move. Mercifully, it finished at nine o'clock. She was going to go up and have a bath, when *Starsky and Hutch* came on, so she settled back into the sofa and watched that. She liked both Paul Michael Glaser and David Soul. It was a good episode. Lots of car chases.

When it finished the announcer said that *Match of the Day* was coming up after the news, so she turned the television off and went upstairs to run a bath.

She undressed in her room, rummaged about for a towel then crossed the stairway into the back bedroom. She glanced out the window. There was still a little light in the sky, but the first stars were out. The tree looked like a dark monument.

She went over to the bath and tested the water. Happy with the temperature, she closed the partition door and then lowered herself into the tub. She sat upright for a moment, then lay back and breathed out heavily. She looked down at herself and cradled her belly.

She wondered about the sex of the baby and if it would look like her or Tony, or a mix of them both perhaps. She hoped that the child would have Tony's eyes, and his lips, his hair. In fact, she admitted to herself, she wished that their offspring would look just like him. An image of Anthony Lowes in the world, a new version. His legacy made flesh.

There, laying in the bath on that first night in the house on Society Place, Heather finally acknowledged to herself that she felt utterly alone. And terrified of a future without her husband. She began to sob.

∗∗∗

The water had turned cold, but still she lay there, idly working out that when her child would be her age, it would be the year 2000, a new century. She washed her face and was just about to get out, when something made her look at the door. It was firmly shut and the house was silent.

Except, there was somebody on the other side of the door. Listening to her.

She felt utterly sure of it, just as she had earlier that day. It was the unmistakable sense of another presence. Her skin turned to goose flesh again as she stared at the door handle. She stared at it for a long time. It didn't move but she really expected it to.

"Hello?" she said in a cracked voice, immediately wishing she hadn't said anything.

There was no response, but she listened hard.

She began to sing. Wings' *Silly Love Songs* to be exact. That song seemed to be stuck in her head.

Heather got out of the bath and began to dry herself, all the time keeping her eyes on the door handle. She dried her face quickly, not wanting her vision to be obscured for more than a second. Singing the McCartney song seemed to dispel the strong sense of *presence* and suddenly she no longer felt so utterly sure that there was somebody out there.

She wrapped the towel around her and, still singing, she gripped the door handle. She sang louder as she opened the door.

The back bedroom was empty.

Still, she ran from the room, across the stairway, and into her room, flicking on the light and closing the door behind her. The sense of an *other* was gone entirely though and she relaxed a little. She stopped singing, finished drying herself off, put on a vest and underwear and then got into the bed. The sheets were clean and cool. She heard a car turn onto Society Place, passing right beneath her window. She turned on her side and stared at the door.

She didn't fall to sleep for a long time.

CHAPTER THREE

Michael Grant woke and immediately remembered the shit gig he'd had the night before. His band, Candlestick Park, had played a Working Man's Club up in Belper and it had been an unmitigated disaster from start to finish. The clientele had absolutely no interest in hearing *Suffragette City* or *Virginia Plain* and stared at the band—all scruffy longhairs in their mid-20s—with utter contempt. The club was full of an entirely older generation of barrel-chested, 12-pint-a-night men and their toothless, chain-smoking wives (the men all hollered and roared, while the women sat silent and weirdly motionless). Many of these old timers probably thought music died when Elvis went into the army, if indeed they cared a jot for music in the first place. Candlestick Park, a cover band specialising in post-Beatles pop and rock, were doomed from the start.

They'd opened with 10CC's *Rubber Bullets* and it went downhill from there. The first four numbers were met with boos and heckles that intensified after each tune. The crowd only became a little more forgiving when they'd played Mud's *Tiger Feet* ("The knuckle-draggers had seemed to like that one," said Pete afterwards), but then the band completely destroyed any good grace and/or momentum they'd gained by tearing straight into *Smoke on the Water*. There was no coming back from that.

There had nearly been a riot when they struck up Black Sabbath's *Paranoid*. They never even got to finish that one. Halfway through the song, just as Michael was about to go into his pitch perfect Tony Iommi solo, all the power went out to the stage. The management pulled the plug. This led to the first big cheer of the night. The club's owner came on stage and said, "That's enough of that, lads. Clear up and clear off."

There'd been the usual battle to get paid. Pete, the lead singer, got into a slagging match with the club owner, a fat bastard called Len who looked like Ronnie Kray, and it ended up getting quite heated. Paul 'The Stiff' Raisey, the bass player—so called because he moved like he had a rod up his arse—kept telling Paul to "Just leave it, man," (he wanted out of there fast), but Paul wouldn't leave it; he kept on at the owner. The rest of the band packed up the gear as quickly as possible and began taking it all out to the van. Bill, the drummer, had a nightmare dismantling his kit when a couple of the local inbreds got up on stage and started to get a bit confrontational. Michael and The Stiff had to flank Bill and the inbreds backed off a little.

Finally they got loaded up and Bill and The Stiff sat in the van while Michael braved it back inside to get Paul. The place felt very dangerous. Pete however, somehow managed to get paid in full and was striding through the bar like he owned the place. The locals all eyed him with genuine hatred, even the women.

Pete reached Michael and said, "Come on, we best leg it before it all kicks off."

They got in the van and floored it back to Derby.

Another banner night for Candlestick Park. Michael often wondered why he even bothered, but then he'd play a Pink Floyd or Bowie record and the passion would return in full force. He knew, even at times of low ebb, that he felt worse when he wasn't playing music, than when he was. Through all the shit gigs, band politics, financial strain, and constant disappointments, being in Candlestick Park was the centre of his world and without it there wouldn't be much left to hold onto.

Michael's day job was as a painter and decorator, which was a drag for the most part but he made enough to get by. He rented a bedsit in the town centre, and slept on a mattress surrounded by the band's equipment. It'd fell to him to store all the gear as he was the one with the van, and the only one of them who lived on his own. Occasionally Bill would come 'round before a gig and help load up, but more often than not, Michael was left to do it himself, and would have to go and pick the others up, then drive onto wherever that night's gig was.

They mainly played in and around Derbyshire, although they'd gigged in Nottingham a few times, Leicester once or twice, and even a few up in Mansfield and Sheffield. Not too far afield as yet, but then, lugging all the gear around, then driving everywhere, was exhausting work, especially after painting all day. And yet, he did it all for that hour or so he spent on stage. There was nothing like the sound of his guitar blasting out of his Marshall. For that hour he was Jimmy Page, Mick Ronson, David Gilmour. And they were a tight band too. Bill and The Stiff locked in, allowing Michael to fly, and Pete, for all his faults, was one hell of a front man.

They did provincial Working Men's Clubs for the money, but it was the pubs and clubs in the cities where they could really fire on all cylinders. The crowds, mainly a younger set, were far more receptive to their repertoire, so much so, the band was often able to sneak in a few originals. Seeing people dancing and cheering to a song he'd written with Pete in his bedsit was, to Michael, a rush like no other. One particular song, *Hey Girl*, would always go down a storm, to the point where, it had got the band laid once or twice. Even The Stiff copped off after a gig in Chesterfield. He'd had to tell his wife that the van had broken down on the M1 to explain his absence that night.

But the morning after the disastrous Belper gig, Michael lay in bed trying to find the will to actually get up. As it was Saturday, he didn't have anywhere to be, not until the afternoon anyway, so the motivation to move was less than zero. He did sit up and light a cigarette then took long, slow drags and looked to the window. Sunlight spilled in through a gap in the curtains. It was already hot.

He thought about Heather and wondered how she'd been on her first night in her new house. She looked so fragile to him of late, worse now than in the immediate aftermath of Anthony's death. It was as if the grief was slowly digging itself deeper into her, eroding her light—her very essence—from existence. She now looked so small against the world, like a wilting flower.

There was no doubt she was a different girl to the sister he'd grown up with—that girl so carefree and joyous. She was marked now, scarred in a way that could never truly heal, not fully anyway. She looked different too. She'd lost weight, even with the baby on the way, but it was more than that. It was her eyes, they were duller. She had seen and felt too much in such a short space of time and had been left shattered inside. It hurt Michael's heart to think of her in so much pain.

He'd been trying to express all this in a song he'd been writing, but had hit a wall with it. He'd been satisfied with the melody, and its descending chord progression was strong (very Nick Drake, he thought) but exposing so much of his sister's life and pain in a song had seemed like a betrayal of sorts and he'd left it half finished. He hadn't even played it to Pete.

The thought of his sister finally motivated him into action and he prised himself out of bed. He stumbled over to his kitchenette—a fridge, a stove, a sink, all crammed into a corner—and rummaged about, managing to find bacon, eggs and a couple of sausages. He put them all into a plastic bag then threw on some clothes. He checked his hair in the mirror, grabbed his keys and headed out.

***

Heather was up early that morning. She sorted through her clothes, hanging them on an old rail affixed in an alcove then got dressed and went downstairs. She made a cup of tea and sat in the kitchen, the back door open, the sound of birdsong filling the world. After a while she went out on the front and scrubbed her doorstep down. The street was still quiet.

The doorstep cleaned, she tipped the remaining water from her bowl down the gutter then turned to head back inside. Only, she stopped when she noticed her neighbour's front door ajar, and a pair of eyes peering out at her. Her mouth dry, she said, "Hello?" and at first there was no response, just those eyes, unmoving, locked-in on her, but then the door opened a little more and Heather saw a little old woman—knitted jumper, cotton-wool hair, steely gaze and crow's-feet like deep valleys.

"Hello, young lady," said the woman. Her voice was rich and warm and put Heather at ease. She approached her neighbour, offering her hand.

"Hello, I'm Heather Lowes," she said, then added, "I've moved in next door," knowing full well she was stating the obvious.

The old woman took her hand. It felt very small in her own hand, almost like that of a child's. "I'm Mrs Evelyn Green," she said. "Would you like a cup of tea, my dear?"

***

Mrs Green's house smelt a little fusty, and quite strongly of TCP, but it was very neat, not a thing out of place. There was lot of tartan and flowery embroidery; doilies and patterned table runners in abundance. There were knick-knacks everywhere, little porcelain dogs—mainly Yorkshire Terriers—china dolls of various shapes and sizes, and a great many crucifixes, plus other assorted religious figurines and icons. The house had the same layout as Heather's, save for the kitchen doorway, which was on the opposite side to hers, and the stairway ran up from a different part of the kitchen. Mrs Green told Heather to sit at a small table by the back door and then shuffled about the kitchen preparing a pot of tea. She began to boil the kettle on the stove and then delicately placed china cups and saucers on a tray. Heather didn't particularly fancy another cup of tea, the day was already hot, but she didn't want to appear rude. While the kettle was boiling, the biscuit tin also came out, and Mrs Green adjusted the doilies on the table. It was not yet nine o'clock in the morning.

"It's going to be another scorcher today," mused the old woman.

"Yes," Heather agreed. "Last night was stifling."

Mrs Green looked at her then turned back to the stove just as the kettle began to whistle. The hot water was poured into a china teapot and spoons were placed carefully onto the saucers. Heather stood up and offered to carry the tray over but the old woman waved her away, so Heather sat back down. Mrs Green walked across the kitchen and placed the tray in the centre of the table, then sat opposite Heather.

"We'll let that mash in the pot for a minute or two," said Mrs Green. Heather nodded.

A clock was ticking loudly from somewhere in the house but Heather couldn't locate from where. Mrs Green lowered her eyes and opened the biscuit tin.

"I think I've got some chocolate digestives in here somewhere," she said, tilting the tin in Heather's direction. Heather smiled and put her hand in, pulling out a custard cream. "I like these ones," she said, "thank you." She placed it on the edge of her saucer to have with her tea. She felt the old woman's eyes on her again.

"You have a lovely home, Mrs Green," she said, more for something to say than genuine appreciation.

"Thank you," said the old woman. "I've lived in this house a long time. Albert and I moved in here just after we were married in 1927."

"Blimey, that's…what? Fifty years?"

"Yes, forty-nine. Albert and I were together for thirty-seven of those years. He died in 1964. Cancer."

"I'm sorry."

"It's fine, deary. All part of life's rich tapestry."

The old woman poured the tea, first Heather's cup then her own.

"Milk and sugar?" she asked, waving her hand across the milk jug and sugar bowl.

"Yes, thank you," said Heather, and she helped herself to both.

Mrs Green took only milk, then leaned back in her chair and eyed her guest once more.

"You're a very pretty girl," the old woman remarked, and Heather smiled, ran her fingers through her hair, rubbed a hand across her face.

"You're very kind, Mrs Green, but I feel in a bit of state at the moment. I've had to do a lot of work in the house and..."

"Always take the compliment, my dear."

"Yes, sorry, thank you."

Heather took a drink of her tea.

"Are you Mrs Lowes?" asked the woman.

There it was, the question she'd been dreading.

"I am," she said, trying to keep her voice steady.

"Lovely. And you're with child?"

Heather looked at her, astonished. "How?"

"You don't get to my age without knowing a thing or two."

"But..."

"You're glowing with it, my dear."

"I didn't think I was showing yet." She looked down at her belly.

"You are a little," said Mrs Green. "More noticeable on a slight girl like yourself. But it's not your bump that gave you away."

"No?"

"No, it's the way you carry yourself. You move with your right hand always protecting your belly."

"Do I?"

"Yes. I did the same thing when I was with child."

"You have children?"

The old woman lowered her eyes. "Yes. Matthew. He's no longer a child. He's all grown up with a family of his own."

She fell silent. There was something Mrs Green wasn't saying. Heather didn't push her. Instead she drained her cup.

"More tea, Heather?"

"Oh, thank you, Mrs Green, but I really should be getting on. I have so much to do."

"Of course, please don't let me stop you," and in the same breath she asked, "How are you finding the house?"

Heather thought for a moment, then said, "Challenging."

"I'm sure. It has been empty for a number of years."

"It needs a lot of work doing to it," added Heather.

"Well, I'm sure you and your husband will settle in soon enough."

Heather winced, and the tears came on suddenly.

Mrs Green looked shocked. "My dear?"

"It's fine...sorry."

"What is it?"

Heather couldn't answer. She tried to slow her breathing and regain some control.

Mrs Green's expression changed from one of shock and confusion to an awful look of pity. "Oh my dear," she said. "I am sorry."

Heather stood up. "I really must go."

"Yes, of course...but..." The woman put her hand to Heather's elbow. "I'm here...if you need someone...I'm here."

"Thank you, Mrs Green."

"And Heather..."

"Yes?"

The old woman's grip tightened on Heather's arm.

"Make that house your own," she said.

***

As she stepped out of Mrs Green's house, Heather saw her brother's Bedford van turn into Society Place. Heather stood waiting for him, tears streaming down her face. He pulled up outside her house and leapt from the van. He ran to his sister and embraced her.

Michael made a full English breakfast for them both. The works: sausage, eggs, bacon, black pudding, fried tomatoes and fried bread. They ate in silence in Heather's kitchen, the back door open, a warm breeze blowing in. Heather cleared her plate in no time at all and said, "I feel better now. Thank you, Mike."

"No problem," he mumbled, his mouth full.

Heather pushed her plate away from her. "How was your gig?" she asked.

Michael swallowed. "One for the books."

"That good?"

"That bad."

"Oh. Why?"

"They pulled the plug on us."

Heather laughed.

Michael smiled and mopped up his plate with his last piece of fried bread. He said, "How was your first night?"

She took a moment to answer. She thought of the strange episodes in the upstairs rooms but with her belly full and her brother sitting across from her chewing noisily and, moreover, the harsh brightness of the day, it now all felt quite unreal. Had the certainty of a presence in the house simply been a product of grief, exhaustion and nerves, she wondered. A strained mind, an unfamiliar house, and a near crippling anxiety about the future could manifest itself in any number of ways. She had seen nothing, and had heard nothing, for there was nothing, only a frightened and lonely woman in a sad and empty house, and an imagination with its bag of tricks.

She smiled at her brother and said, "I slept like a baby."

"Good," he said, swallowing the last of his food. He leaned back in his chair, patted his stomach and added, "Man, I'm stuffed."

"You make a mean breakfast, Michael Grant."

"Well I'm glad you enjoyed it. Should set you up for the day."

"It sure will."

"And what are your plans today?"

"Well," she pondered. "I got a lot done yesterday. I suppose…"

"It is looking nice," he said, scanning the kitchen.

"I suppose I should make a start on the cellar. It's a right tip down there."

"You wanna hand? I've got band practice at four, but I'm good till then."

"No, I should be alright, Mike, you've done enough."

He looked at her. "I'm here, y'know, Heather. You don't have to do everything on your own. I want to help."

She bit her lip.

"I better get all this washed up," she said, and began clearing the table.

Michael watched her go to the sink and rinse the plates. He got up and looked to the cellar door that lay between the kitchen and the front room. He walked over and opened it. Heather turned from the sink and watched him. He turned on the light and groaned.

"Oh, Heather," he said. "You weren't wrong, it's a tip."

Junk was piled all the way up the stairs. "And it stinks down there."

He turned off the light and closed the door.

"You're not going down there, Heather."

"What?"

"No, Heather. Not in your condition."

"Oh, come on."

"No, I'm serious. You could strain yourself, or fall...God knows what."

He walked over to her. "Look," he said, "I can't do tomorrow or Monday 'cause I've got a job on, but I'll come back on Tuesday and I'll get all that cleared out. I'll see if I can get Paul to help us."

"Okay, Mike, thanks."

"Hey, what are big brothers for?"

***

In the afternoon Heather went to Presto's and did the big shop. While she was in there she noticed a sign saying that they were currently hiring more cashiers. She inquired about the position with a middle-aged lady in a Presto's t-shirt milling about the aisles. The lady led Heather over to an empty till, rifled about beneath the cashiers' stool and pulled out an application form. "Fill this out," she said, "and drop it back in."

Heather thanked her and then carried on shopping.

It ended up being quite a big shop indeed and Heather had to struggle back to Society Place carrying five heavy plastic bags in the eighty degree heat. The bags cut into her fingers and she had to stop often, put the bags down, and catch her breath.

She passed Normanton Arboretum and peered through the iron railings to watch the kids playing out on the grass, and pretty girls in tight shorts sunning themselves, and families out walking, eating ice creams and kicking footballs about with their children. She noticed one young family, a mother and a father, not much older than herself, pushing a pram beneath the long shadows of trees. She watched them for a long while, before they disappeared from view.

Finally she made it back to Society Place and found Rafferty and his friends out on the street again. An ice cream van was parked up and there was a line of kids queuing up. Several kids had ice cream around their faces and dripping down their arms. Every one of them looked sweaty and grubby, and every one of them looked like they were in their element.

Rafferty spotted Heather and waved. She nodded back. He noticed her bags and came running over. "Lemme help," he said, and took one of the bags from her. She made sure he got the lightest bag.

"Thank you, Raff."

"That's okay," he said. He also had a sticky, grubby little face. "I've just had an ice cream."

"That's good. Did you enjoy it?"

"Oh yes," he beamed. "I even had strawberry sauce on mine."

"You're a very lucky boy."

They walked past the ice cream van and towards her house. Things were a little quieter this end of the street.

"Mum gave me the money for the ice cream and told me not to tell dad."

Heather looked down at the little boy. "Is that bag okay, Raff? Not too heavy."

"No, Heather, I can do it. I'm strong."

Heather smiled. 'Yes…yes you are."

When they got to Heather's door, she put her bags down by the front step, and Raff did the same, then he stepped back from the house. Heather turned the key and opened the door then she noticed Rafferty looking up at her bedroom window. Heather crouched down, so to be at the boy's eye level, and said, "Rafferty."

He looked at her. "Yes?"

"Why did you run off yesterday…when you saw me up in my room?"

The boy looked unsure of what to say. He glanced up at the window again then lowered his eyes to the ground.

"It's okay, Raff," she said. "You can tell me."

He looked at her again, licked his lips, then said, "The man who was stood behind you. I didn't like his face."

CHAPTER FOUR

On her second night in 2 Society Place, Heather went to bed early. In an already scorching summer, the day had been, according to the evening news, the hottest on record (Michael Fish said it'd reached 35.9 °C (96.6 °F) in some parts of the country) and Heather had thought a few times that she could've fried an egg on her skin. An expression of her mother's.

She'd kept busy though; she cleaned the windows, swept the yard, then refitted several of the loose or missing roof slates on the outhouse (many slates were hot to the touch). She fixed the roof from a small wooden ladder she'd discovered by the back gate. The sweat dripped off her. She drank large glasses of water—glass after glass—and often dipped her head under the cold tap. The sun was blinding in the sky, and the day seemed to positively hum with the heat. Heather got a headache from the constant squinting.

In the evening, Heather ate light: a salad with a few new potatoes. Her appetite was virtually non-existent, but she knew she had better eat for the sake of her strength. She sat in a cold bath for a while, which felt wonderful, after which she dressed in shorts and a light vest top and went back down stairs to watch telly. There was nothing on. She kept getting up to flick between BBC1 and 2—the choice being *Jim'll Fix It* or golf. She still couldn't tune ITV in. In the end, she turned the TV off and went and sat out on the back-step, the early evening sky still a cloudless, piecing blue. The sun was low; a magical golden light on everything. It was still very hot. It was going to be another sweltering night. She couldn't remember the last time it had rained. A hosepipe ban had been in place since late June and newscasters and the papers were constantly advising people to save on water. Reservoirs were drying up and there was footage on the news of families filling tubs of water at standpipes. Heather had even seen one government official suggesting people take baths with a friend. There had also been reports of people dying of heatstroke, particularly elderly folk, and several animals had also died—mainly dogs locked in cars. Plus, there were the ladybirds.

The news referred to them as a plague. The British Entomological and Natural History Society estimated that there were in excess of twenty-three billion of the little bugs, and they were indeed everywhere. According to one report, which Heather had half watched at Tom and Jean's one night before she'd moved, the hot, dry summer had all but wiped out the ladybirds' food source, aphids—greenfly basically—and so the plague were hungry and had smothered the country looking for nutrition. Heather had herself seen great moving clumps of ladybirds up posts and scuttling across pavements, masses so thick it was almost impossible not to tread on them. The crunch underfoot was horrible.

Coastal towns had been utterly besieged and locals and holidaymakers alike were attacked daily. The thirsty creatures had taken to swarming people, rehydrating themselves on human sweat. They were also attracted to ice cream, and Heather had seen one news report showing a young man holding aloft an ice lolly, his arm completely covered, pulsing with the things. There had even been reports of people being bitten, which Heather had found hard to believe, until her brother's drummer, Bill, showed her several tiny dots running up the inside of his arm.

She'd often thought, as the days grew hotter and hotter and the plague intensified, that it all seemed like something out of a horror film. Michael had even said at one point, "This summer feels positively apocalyptic."

Heather had winced when he said it.

***

She got up off the step and closed the back door. The sun had dipped behind houses and the golden light had turned to a hazy red. She sat at her kitchen table and spent half an hour or more trying to fill in the application form for the Presto's job. She managed her name, address, date of birth and a couple of other boxes, then sat staring blankly at the paper for ages. The light shifted and grew darker. Finally she admitted defeat and went upstairs to bed. It was not yet ten o'clock.

She didn't think about what Rafferty had said to her until she got into bed.

***

When she woke it was fully dark. She was disorientated, her head fuzzy, her mouth dry. The house was very still.

She couldn't remember falling asleep. She recalled laying down, staring at her bedroom door, and turning Rafferty's words over in her mind.

I didn't like his face.

She figured she must've gone out like a light (another expression of her mother's), and she also had no idea how long she'd been asleep for, although it felt late.

There was one thing she was very clear on, however. She needed to pee really badly. In fact, she was bursting to go.

She'd read a pamphlet at the doctors recently explaining how the uterus can often press against the bladder during early pregnancy, causing considerable discomfort, and boy, they weren't kidding. It felt like a dead weight had been dropped onto her pelvic floor.

She grimaced as she got up out of bed. Stomping about the room she located her slippers then was out the door and down the stairs with some urgency. She crossed the kitchen, fumbled with the key, threw open the back door, and stepped out into the night. It was very warm still and the moon bright. She rushed into the toilet and sat down, astonished when only a small trickle of pee came out.

She sat there for a long while, waiting for the sensation of wanting to wee had passed. A little more came out of her, but nothing to warrant the discomfort she felt. She kicked the outhouse door open and sat looking up at the stars. The night was very clear, the sky opened up in all its majesty.

Eventually the pressure subsided and she felt some relief. She remained seated and continued to stare at the night sky. She caught sight of something and shot forward, straining to see what it was, nearly falling off the toilet in the process. It was a shooting star, the briefest of light, and Heather gasped in wonder. She had never seen one before.

She got up off the toilet, pulled her shorts up, and stepped out into the yard, her eyes fixed to the sky. A breeze kicked up, rustling through the tall tree—a dark mass against the sky—and Heather watched for more shooting stars. There were none, but it didn't stop her from soaking in the celestial magic show above. She found she was holding her belly, and for a moment, a brief moment, she felt complete peace.

All that changed however when she looked to the house, and saw, through the kitchen window, the pitch black opening of the stairway. She felt the hairs rise on her neck and shivered involuntarily. She shook her head, mainly at herself, wondering why she was being so irrational. Yet, there it was, in the pit of her stomach, a sudden and unmistakable rush of fear. She did not want to go back into the house.

She turned away and looked up at the moon. It was a waxing gibbous, very bright, a halo of light around it. She remembered something her mother used to say, *ring around the moon means rain soon*, and wondered if it meant that the summer was about to break. She hoped so.

She looked to the vastness of the cosmos. In all that space, she thought, how could there be something on my stairs? She laughed at this then turned back to the house and all the humour left her.

The darkness of the stairway opening was dense and somewhat unreal against the moon shadows in the kitchen. It was like a void.

"This is ridiculous," she muttered, not believing for a second that what she was sensing was ridiculous in the slightest. Another phrase suddenly came to her: *spooky action at a distance*. She couldn't place where she'd heard it, or even, what it really meant, but something about the phrase struck her as true. She had neither seen nor heard anything in her new house, and yet, the sense of a *presence* was unmistakable. Not all the time, *it* seemed to come and go, but she was certain it was in there now. Waiting.

She wondered what to do. She looked across to the bedroom window of Mrs Green's house. All in darkness. There was no sound coming from anywhere. No cars, no lights, no distant voices, nothing, just the slight breeze whispering through the tall tree. This truly was the dead of night. She wondered what the time actually was and approached the back door, peering in to catch a glimpse of the kitchen clock. It was three o'clock in the morning.

She took another step, looking around the back door to the stairway opening across the kitchen. The house, like the night, was silent, but that wasn't to say there was nobody stood on the stairs.

Heather stepped into the kitchen, found the light switch and flicked it on. The harsh light made her wince. Then she began to hum. *Silly Love Songs* again, soon picking up the words and singing softly. She took a step toward the stairway.

About halfway across the kitchen she suddenly smelt something. It was faint at first, then burst into a fowl scent that made Heather gag. It smelt a little like rotten eggs, something gone very bad. She stood motionless for a moment. The smell, she realised, wasn't coming from the stairs, but seemed to be emanating from the cellar. She turned her head, but as soon as she looked in the direction of the cellar, the smell disappeared. Not even a trace of its stench lingered. So sudden was its disappearance Heather questioned whether the smell had even been there at all. Was this a game, she wondered. Was it purposely trying to make her doubt her senses?

She picked up singing *Silly Love Songs* and stepped into the stairway.

Stood on the bottom step, she looked up. The stairway lay in darkness but she could make out her bedroom door, which she'd left ajar. She closed her eyes when she turned on the light. She felt the sudden illumination behind her eyelids, but didn't open them at first. She heard her blood pumping and realised she was shaking.

She opened her eyes.

Drab walls, dim light, no sound.

She went to sing, but choked. She sensed someone stood behind her.

A noise came out of her throat and she ran up the stairs, not daring to look back.

It followed her all the way up. Of that she was certain.

She got into her bedroom and slammed the door shut.

The *presence* didn't follow her inside.

Instead the sense of *it* being there, on the other side of the door, quickly faded away, and she felt sure she was alone again.

Heather got into bed, breathing heavily. Her heart thumped against her chest and she was clammy with sweat.

She didn't get to sleep again that night, only lay there until morning, staring at her bedroom door, wondering if she was going crazy or if she truly had moved into a haunted house.

***

The next day she walked into town and bought a bedpan from Woolworths.

CHAPTER FIVE

Rafferty wanted to climb the tree. He'd been thinking about it all summer, ever since he'd broken up from school. Truth be told, he'd thought about it long before then but the impulse to conquer the tree came on seriously strong as the six weeks holidays hit. He could almost think of nothing else.

Foolishly he'd expressed this desire to his mother one afternoon, and had been told in no uncertain terms that if he went anywhere near the tree he'd be in serious trouble. She'd said, "You could fall and break something, or worse, smash the windows in Mr Newbold's greenhouse."

Mr Newbold's greenhouse did stand beneath several thick branches and one wrong move could indeed cause some serious damage but Raff wasn't overly concerned about that. Nor was he that concerned about breaking a bone. His need to climb the tree was too great and far outweighed any trouble he may find himself in. He just knew that the glory in reaching those top branches was worth any punishment.

And so it was, with his father at work and his mother at the shops, young Rafferty Gilroy decided that he was done plotting and scheming, he was just going to climb the sucker.

Gnarled roots poked through broken concrete at the bottom of Rafferty's backyard.

His dad had taken a couple of panels out of the fence in order to negotiate the tree's network through the earth. Mr Newbold's fence had also been accommodated to allow for the tree's steady encroachment. It was a beast of a tree. Its trunk was deep with fissures and low hanging branches stretched themselves out across several of the surrounding backyards, Rafferty's and Mr Newbold's included.

Raff unlatched the back gate and stepped out into the jitty. The ground here was uneven, with patchy grass, weeds, and rubbish bags. This narrow pathway ran along the back of every house on Society Place, before joining a second, wider path along Silver Hill Road. Kids often played out here, particularly the older boys. There were plenty of places to huddle out of sight and have a smoke and look at dirty magazines.

The trunk of the ash tree stood back from the path, beside someone's garden shed across the way, but its roots tore across the earth making the jitty hazardous after dark, and its branches hung low and long. Low enough to climb up onto.

Raff wiped his forehead with the back of his hand. It was blazing hot again and for a brief moment Raff considered not tackling the tree, at least until the summer cooled down a little, but then decided that now was as good a time as any. His mother rarely left him on his own, and so he needed to take full advantage of this brief gift of freedom.

He approached the nearest branches and looked up. From this angle there was no sky, only the deep green and aged brown of the tree itself; a domed canopy of leaves and branches, beckoning young Rafferty into its secret world.

He looked back down the jitty. All was quiet, so he reached up and grabbed the lowest branch and pulled himself up, digging one foot into the trunk to give him some purchase. With a great deal of effort and a lot of huffing and puffing, Raff pulled himself up and onto the branch. He grazed his knee, causing him to take a sharp intake of breath. He gritted his teeth and positioned himself on the branch. It swayed beneath his weight.

He sat for a moment and concentrated on maintaining his balance, and looked down at his knee. There were red scratch marks, a little blood breaking the surface, and he had to stop himself from blubbing. Maybe shorts and a t-shirt were not the best attire for tree climbing. He thought about jumping back down and going in to change but the heat was so stifling that a stitch more on his body would just be unbearable, especially up in the tree. And anyway, he was here now and determined to not let the great gnarly old thing get the better of him at the first branch. He wasn't a baby anymore, he was nine years old. Big enough and strong enough to master the art of tree climbing. Phil Ingram from Silver Hill Road had done it, said he'd reached the top, and he was four months younger than Raff, so he had to go on.

With great care he stood up, wrapping his arms around the trunk for support. Beads of sweat poured down his face, stinging his eyes.

He adjusted his feet and took one hand away from the tree in order to wipe his face. He pressed the back of his hand into his eyes, one to the other. The branch swayed and he shot his hand back to the trunk, his heart thumping.

He grabbed onto the next branch and hoisted himself up. The density of the tree enveloped him and the jitty disappeared from view. This worried Raff, but still he continued on, moving upwards, his footing surer, his lifts more graceful by degrees. He scraped his legs and arms some more, and the leaves made him itch, but he tried his best to ignore all that and concentrated on the climb.

Feeling he was really very high, he stopped to catch his breath. He felt grubby; the sweat and dirt, and the stings from where he'd cut himself made him long to jump into a bath of cold water and then have his hurts covered with Germolene (he loved the smell). He knew that as soon as his mum laid eyes on him he'd be in for it but he was past the point of no return now.

He continued up onto the next branch, and clung onto the trunk. He decided that he'd gone high enough. He looked down and he felt his head go all spinny and he had to lower himself and sit on the branch. It hurt his bottom and he had to shuffle about, the branch bouncing and rustling beneath him. The ground looked a long, long way away.

There was a thin branch in front of him and he bent this downwards in order to peer through the tree. His eyes levelled with the back bedroom window of the pretty lady's house, the one who had just moved in. The window lay in darkness, yet no curtains appeared to be drawn. It seemed strange against the harsh light of the sun.

Raff stared at the window for a long time, unsure as to why exactly. There was something about the house he didn't like. Always had been—he never played down that end of the street, not if he could help it—but since the lady had moved in, this sense of a *wrongness* with the house felt more real. Just looking at the place made him feel tingly, the nape of his neck all a-prickle and alert. He couldn't understand these feelings but thought that maybe it was because he didn't like the face of the man the pretty lady lived with.

He shivered, despite the heat, and thought of something his mum said about shivering—that it is because people were walking over your grave—and he shivered again. He figured he'd better get down and get cleaned up before his mum got back, and readied himself for the climb down, when something caught his eye in the room beyond. A movement. A figure crossing the window.

Raff bent the branch down further and leant forward. From that point on, everything that happened to young Rafferty Gilroy happened very fast. First, a pale and painfully gaunt face burst at the window. Burst being the right word as one moment there was dark, the other there was a face, as quick as light. It was disembodied, a face only, and Rafferty had no time in which to register its features. The only thing he did register before the branch he was holding snapped in two was that its eyes—eyes like great big black marbles—were looking straight at him.

Then down he went, and to young Rafferty it felt like he was falling forever. The thinner branches snapped under his weight, but the larger ones made their stand, sending the boy bouncing down and across from one branch to another and another and another, like a human pinball machine, only with bumpers and kickers and slingshots that could bite and scratch. Rafferty's skin was lacerated. His eyelids were clawed at. A twig rammed itself into his mouth. He heard a snap different from the snapping of the tree, an internal snap: the snap of bone. However, he didn't scream during the fall; he had no breath to do so.

He banged his head on the final branch, a thump that shook his brain in its skull, and as the tree spat his limb body out into the jitty, Rafferty's final thought before he passed out was that he was going to die and end up like the things that lived in the pretty lady's house.

CHAPTER SIX

Michael, Heather and Paul Raisey peered down into the cellar. The smell was immediate. It was the smell of age; of damp and mould and of wet, festering fabrics. It was not the smell Heather had caught two nights previous; the sudden, ephemeral stink of rotten eggs. It was simply the emanations of an old and forgotten place.

Heather flicked the light on but it did little to illuminate the cellar. The stairway was blocked by piles of dust sheets, a broken up rocking chair, old tins of paint, a metal tool box (opened and empty), and other such odds and sods. There was a doorless frame at the bottom of the stairs that led to a room off to the right, but until the junk was shifted, the stairs were impassable.

Michael sighed and looked at Paul. The Stiff raised his eyebrows. Michael then looked at his sister and said, "You better put the kettle on, Heather. Think we're gonna be here a while."

"Will do," said Heather and stepped into the kitchen. She lit a burner on the stove and filled the kettle up. "You have sugar, Paul?"

He shouted up from the cellar stairs. "Three, please, me duck."

She put the kettle on the stove and listened to Paul and her brother rummaging about.

She heard her brother say to Paul, "We better clear these sheets first," and there was movement, a lot of huffing and puffing, and the clatter of something very noisily tumbling down the stairs.

Heather rushed to the cellar door. "You alright?"

Mike and Paul were coming up, carrying armfuls of mouldy dust sheets.

"Ay," said Mike. "Move out—"

She stepped to the side as they both rushed past her. They went through the front room and straight out onto the street. They dropped the sheets on the road by the back doors of Mike's Bedford van. Both of them began to cough. Mike spat into the gutter and Paul sneezed three times in quick succession. Heather wrinkled her nose and returned to making the tea.

The boys came back in and went down the cellar, clattering and banging about, muttering swear words and groaning and coughing. Heather rinsed three mugs and lifted the squealing kettle off the stove. She threw three teabags into the pot, poured the water in then popped the lid on to mash. She went through the motions, her mind elsewhere.

She'd woken that Tuesday morning feeling incredibly refreshed, after having the best night's sleep since moving in. Not one disturbance all night. She had gone to bed at ten and slept right through. She even dreamt of Tony. He held her hand as they crossed a narrow bridge. He was dressed in the suit he'd worn on their wedding day. He looked so handsome.

The warmth of his presence stayed with her on waking and it made her feel happy. Genuinely happy. She'd gone downstairs, turned on the radio and sang along to *Don't Go Breaking My Heart* by Elton John and Kiki Dee at the top of her voice as she made herself scrambled eggs and toast.

The experiences she'd had since moving in, particularly on the Sunday night, now felt very distance and very unreal. That night in particular—the night she'd gone down to use the outside loo and had felt the presence on the stairs—now seemed like a dream. A fever dream perhaps; the manifestations of a tired and overwrought mind. After all, she'd told herself, she was a twenty-four year old widow, with child, looking at an uncertain future in a strange house, racked with loneliness and grief—what mind could carry such weight? The loneliness was often the hardest to take. She had nobody now, other than Michael and he had his own life, his own dreams, and she couldn't continue to badger him for this and for that.

She told herself that she had simply impressed all her worry and distress on the house; the strange and new thing in her life. The house that should have been a home for her and Tony and their baby. The house that still felt like it belonged to somebody else.

Yet, on that Tuesday morning, all these anxieties were pushed far back. Buried deep. She felt better than she could remember feeling for a very, very long time. Michael had even commented on how good she looked when he and Paul arrived. He'd said she was 'glowing' and she smiled at this. A genuine smile.

She took the lads their tea and they had a breather out on the front, both of them leaning up against the van. They'd brought up a few of the rusty old tins of paint. Heather sat on her front step and watched them. Kids were playing out on the street, but she couldn't see Rafferty.

She turned to Michael and said, "I've got an interview for a job at twelve."

"Great," he said, "Where at?"

"Presto's. The shop on Normanton Road."

"Well, that's wonderful, sis."

"It's only part time, but should keep the wolf from the door a little. If I get it, that is."

"You will," said Michael. Heather smiled. The one thing she really loved about her brother was his eternal optimism.

He finished his tea and handed her his mug. Paul did the same and smiled at her. He never said much.

"Right, we better be getting on," said Michael. "Lot of stuff to clear."

Heather stood up, holding all three mugs. "Yes, thank you so much, you two."

"It's not a bother," said Michael.

"Yeah, no trouble, duck." The Stiff called everyone duck. He was proper Derby.

"Well I better go and get ready for my interview."

"We'll crack on."

"Michael?"

"Yeah?"

"Really, thank you."

Michael smiled at her. "Be off with you."

He kissed her forehead then crossed the front room and went back into the cellar. The Stiff gave her twitchy grin then followed Mike down.

Heather went upstairs, the light within her still strong.

***

While Paul and her brother got on with her cellar, Heather walked in the stifling heat to Presto's for her noon interview. She was sweaty and grubby by the time she got there and had to ask for a large glass of water before she could be interviewed. The store manager and one of his underlings sat across from her and asked a series of standard questions—*what do you feel you could bring to your role as a check out supervisor? Do you have any previous experience of working in retail? Do you feel you work well within a team?* and so on.

Heather answered everything as best she could but she knew she was just going through the motions. She told them what they wanted to hear and smiled and kept eye contact and made no mention of being pregnant. The store manager was a portly fellow named Craig Sullivan. He seemed pleasant enough, if a little odd and unsure of himself. His underling on the other hand was a middle-aged woman named Carol who had rather large bosoms and a face like a smacked arse. She was the 'team leader' apparently but made no effort to be pleasant or civil to Heather. She asked most of the questions. Heather had met people like Carol before and just knew that she'd have to watch her step with her.

The interview lasted for fifteen minutes and Heather didn't feel particularly good about her chances. She felt her answers were laboured, unconvincing to her own ears. She was hot and distracted. Her clothes stifled her. She wore her best skirt and a plain white shirt. The back of the shirt stuck to her skin and her bra dug into her sides. She was irritable and tried desperately to keep her shortening temper in check. Carol made this something of a challenge with her abrupt manner and judging eyes.

So at the end of the interview Heather was astonished when Mr Sullivan offered her the job on the spot and asked if she could start on Friday. She gave an unequivocal YES and then Carol cut in and said her hours would be 10a.m. to 3p.m., Tuesday to Saturday, and that her hourly rate would be £1.29—£32 per week, before tax.

Before she left Presto's, Heather bought herself a chicken to cook for that night's dinner and treated herself to some chocolate.

***

The ice cream van was parked up on Society Place again. A few kids were sat on the kerb, scabs on knees; the stain of ice lollies around their mouths, hair matted and grubby. Summer kids, deep in the bliss of the six week's holidays. Rafferty wasn't among them and

Heather thought it strange that she hadn't seen him around for a few days.

As she passed the ice cream man she caught his attention and asked if he was about to move onto another street. He was sat at the wheel reading a paper and turned to speak to her. "I'll be here for another five minutes, love. You want me to hang on for you?"

"Please," she said. "I'll just pop this shopping in and then I'll be back out."

"Right you are," said the ice cream man and went back to his paper.

She thought Mike and Paul would both appreciate an ice cream after lugging all that junk up from the cellar and she knew she could sure demolish one.

The back of Mike's Bedford van was stacked full of crap. Her front door was open and as she stepped inside she saw there were dirty footprints all over the carpet.

"Mike," she shouted. "I'm back."

She heard him coming up the cellar stairs, and for a moment, a very brief moment, the thought came to her that it wasn't Michael or Paul coming up the stairs, but someone else. The hairs on the nape of her neck bristled but then Mike did appear. He was sweaty and filthy, but that wasn't all. He looked stricken. She knew something was very wrong.

She dropped the shopping bag. "What?"

He looked at her.

"Michael, what is it?"

He swallowed then said, "You better come down here and take a look."

CHAPTER SEVEN

The first thing Heather saw were the markings on the walls. Every inch was covered in strange symbols, crude drawings of various acts of sexual depravity, of monstrous looking creatures and men and women with oversized sexual parts intertwined in all sorts of positions. Some were chalk drawings, some were painted. Also, there looked to be mud up some of the walls but it stank badly and Heather thought that it perhaps wasn't mud at all.

Her breath was taken and she couldn't get any words out. Michael and Paul stood either side of her, neither of them spoke. There was a grate in a corner of the ceiling that led up to the pavement. It allowed a great shaft of light to pour into the cellar. Heather stepped further into the room and that's when she saw the bones.

There were animal bones all over the floor in one corner. There was the skull of a cat, and another that was perhaps a small dog, or a fox. Heather gagged and held her hand to her mouth. Michael came to her side, his hands gripping her shoulders, steadying her.

"It's okay, Heather," he said. "We'll get all this shifted. It's probably just some sicko's idea of a joke."

She lowered her hand and looked at him. "This doesn't look like a joke."

"I shouldn't have brought you down here," he said. "I was just a little overwhelmed but don't worry, sis, this will all be gone. Me and Paul are gonna clear the lot and give it a good clean down."

"Are we?" said Paul.

Michael scowled at him. "Yes, we are. Look, Poppy, it's okay. It's nothing. There's a lot of weird people into a lot of bullshit, that's all. Ever since that *Exorcist* film came out, people have been into a lot of stupid shit. It's bollocks, Heather. Believe me."

Heather didn't say anything. She simply continued staring at the walls. The mouth of a demon here, the copulation of monsters there. She approached the front wall, the one with the grate above and looked up into the light. She heard the kids playing out on the street. Directly in front of her was the crude drawing of a man with a two mouths where his eyes should be—the teeth sharp and grinning—and in place of where his mouth should be, an upside down cross. An inverted cross. A most unholy cross.

She turned to her brother. She noticed Paul looking decidedly uncomfortable behind him. "Whoever lived here before me," she said, "certainly had quite an imagination."

"That's one word for it," said Paul.

"Listen," said Heather. "I'll hire someone to clean all this up. I can't expect you two to do it. Beside, you've got to go soon, haven't you?"

"What time is it?"

"Getting on for two, maybe later. You got to go at four, right?"

"We have, but…"

"It's fine. Like you said, this is all bullshit, right. They're just drawings."

"Those aren't," said Paul, pointing to the pile of bones.

"No," said Heather, looking down at them. "No, they're not. If you could remove those before you go, that would be really great."

"We will," said Michael. "But you can't go hiring some cleaner for the walls, you haven't got the money. I'll come back tomorrow and wash them down."

"I can do it, Michael."

"I don't want you to."

"Why not? I'm not a girl anymore, Mike. Washing some smut off a cellar wall is nothing compared to what I've been through this year."

Michael looked away then finally said, "Okay, but we'll move the bones."

***

The boys had a rest first. Heather bought them all ice creams and they sat out on the kerb and enjoyed the sunshine. Heather told Michael that she'd gotten the job at Presto's and he was genuinely pleased for her. She could tell though that he was worried about her. There was a sadness to him when he looked at her now. He'd always been a protective brother when they were young, but in recent years that had gotten to be less and less a factor, until Tony died that is. After that, he'd become a little different with her. He handled her as if she were a fragile doll, a thing that could be broken very easily. He was sweet and kind, and was always there for her, but sometimes she thought some tough love might be better for her. Still, she saw she couldn't have done without him these past few months, especially now she had moved into Society Place.

She sat eating her ice cream, watching the kids on the street kicking a ball around, hearing Bob Marley drift from an open window a few doors down. She looked across to the grate in the pavement beneath her front window, the grate that led down to her cellar. Whatever had gone on down there had not been good. An understatement, she thought. Michael had been right, in the wake of *The Exorcist* interest in the Devil and the occult had certainly hit the zeitgeist, and it seemed every man and his dog had done a Ouija board or dabbled in séances and the like. Even Michael's hero Jimmy Page was said to be a black magician and was a disciple of Aleister Crowley. Heather had read that he even owned Crowley's old house up in Scotland and did all sorts of dark magickal rituals. Magick with a k.

In the media there didn't seem to be a week went by without some mention of a haunting, or a possession, or a poltergeist somewhere in the country. It was a craze, a fad, and yet...and yet, Heather knew her house was haunted. The certainty ebbed and flowed, but deep down she knew something was in the house with her. What troubled her more was that whatever that something was, it didn't *feel* like it was good, and the discovery in the cellar had done nothing to ease this feeling, to say the least. But these were night thoughts, deep down thoughts, not thoughts for a bright sunny day, eating ice creams and listening to Bob Marley. Yet, the thoughts came all the same. There was a sense of normality, but it was a veneer. Things were far from normal. It seemed that when it came to the house on Society Place, normality didn't apply.

They finished their ice creams and Michael and Paul went back down the cellar. Heather licked her fingers and went over to talk to the kids playing football.

***

They reapplied their gloves and set to work. They threw the bones into a large black bag. It was not pleasant work. Michael felt beads of sweat running down his forehead and had to keep wiping it with his arm. They got rid of the skulls first. A cat, a dog, a fox perhaps.

"This is like devil worship stuff, aint it?" said Paul.

"Keep your voice down," said Michael. "I don't want Heather to hear...but yes, it certainly looks that way. What else could all this mean?"

"I don't know."

They threw the last of the bones into the black bag and tied it up.

"I'll just go and chuck this on the van," said Michael. "Can you just move that board, mate? Lay it flat or something? It doesn't look very safe."

Michael picked up the bag of bones and left the cellar. Paul looked at the piece of board leant up against one of the walls and sighed.

***

There were three boys and one girl out kicking the ball and generally tear-arsing around the street. Heather approached them and smiled. They saw her and one of the boys picked up the ball and waited for her to speak. He was a ginger-haired lad with a face-full of freckles, a Superman t-shirt and cut-off jeans. He carried himself differently from the others and Heather surmised that he was the leader of this small band of tearaways.

"Hello, my name's Heather. I've just moved in down the street."

"We know," said the ginger-haired lad. "We've seen you."

The girl in the group—pigtails and wide eyes—said, "How'd you like the house?"

The two other lads sniggered at this which put Heather on the back-foot.

"It's…fine," she said, frowning. "I just wanted to ask if you've seen Rafferty at all? I've not seen him about for a few days."

"Oh, didn't you hear?" said the girl.

"No."

"He fell out a tree and broke his arm."

"Really? Is he okay?"

One of the other boys chimed in, "I heard he broke both arms and a rib."

"Nah," said the ginger-haired lad. "It was a couple of ribs and both his legs."

"Oh dear," said Heather. "Is he at home?"

"No, still in the hospital," said the girl. "It sounds bad."

"Yes, I'm sure. What tree did he fall out of?"

"The big one, out back," said the ginger-haired lad, motioning to the houses. "In the gardens…"

She knew he meant the ash tree.

"What number house does he live at? Is it number 9? I'd like to speak to his parents and see how he is."

"Yeah, number 9," said the girl. "You pregnant, Miss?"

Heather held his belly and said, "Yes, I am."

"That's nice," said the girl.

***

Michael came back down the cellar stairs to find Paul at the bottom waiting for him.

"What?" said Michael.

"You've gotta see this…"

Paul went back into the cellar and Michael followed. Paul had moved the board, laying it flat on the ground. What it revealed was an opening. At first Michael thought it might be an old coal shoot, but then he realised that it was a tunnel. A dark opening, large enough to fit a man inside, if he was to crawl through.

They approached it.

Michael said, "How far does it go?"

"I don't know. At least to next door, maybe further. Maybe the entire street."

"That's ridiculous."

"Is it? No more ridiculous than a cellar full of bones and occult drawings."

Michael didn't say anything.

"What are you going to tell Heather?"

"I don't know," said Michael. "I need to think."

Above they heard Heather re-enter the house, her footfalls over their heads. Michael rushed across the cellar and shouted up just as she appeared at the top of the stairs.

"We're nearly done here. Pop the kettle on would you—we'll have a brew before we head off."

"Righto," said Heather. She went into the kitchen.

Michael went back into the cellar. "Let's put the board back up."

"What?"

"Just grab the end will ya, we can't have Heather see this. She's got enough to think about."

They lifted the board back over the hole then Michael kicked his foot against it.

"We need something to stack against this," he said.

"We've just cleared everything," said Paul.

Michael sighed, then said, "Run up to the van and get my drill."

Paul nodded and left the cellar.

While he waited, Michael looked around at the walls and shook his head. Two goblin-like creatures were suckling from a fat woman's breasts, surrounded by a great many symbols. Michael had no idea what they meant, nor did he care to learn. He just wanted it all gone. Gone and forgotten.

Paul returned with his drill box and took over holding the board flat against the wall while Michael sourced a plug. Luckily there was one at the bottom of the stairs and the lead just about reached. He began drilling a pilot hole, deep into the brick work. The noise was very loud. Once one hole was drilled, he released his finger from the trigger and the drill came to a stop. He could hear Heather calling him from the top of the stairs.

"Michael! What are you doing?"

"It's alright," he shouted up. "There's just some loose brickwork down here. I'm just boarding it up as a temporary measure. Don't come down."

Michael looked at Paul, who raised his eyebrows. He continued with the pilot holes, drilling three more in each corner of the board, and filled them with wall plugs. Then he changed the bit and screwed the board against the wall with three inch screws. That done, he stood back.

"I'm going to have to come back tomorrow and brick that hole up."

CHAPTER EIGHT

That evening Heather walked down to number 9 and knocked on the door. There was no answer at first, so she knocked again. This time the door opened. A little.

A woman appeared. She seemed to be in her late twenties/early thirties and had long straight black hair that parted in the middle, framing her face. She was very beautiful, but looked tired, very tired. There was no spark to her eyes, just a dull, almost lifeless expression. Dead eyes, thought Heather. It occurred to her that the woman might be stoned.

"Hello, my name is Heather Lowes and I've just moved into number 2."

"Yeah?"

"Well, your son, Rafferty…"

"What did he do?"

"Nothing. No, it's nothing like that. I heard he had a fall and I just wanted to wish him well."

The woman narrowed her eyes.

"I do hope he's alright?" asked Heather.

"He was climbing that tree out back."

"Yes, I heard. Is he okay?"

"He'll live, I suppose. He broke his right arm and cracked a rib. He's covered in bruises."

"Oh, that's just awful. You must have been so worried?"

The woman didn't respond.

"Well…" said Heather, trying to say something to fill the silence. "Give him my best. I do hope he gets better soon."

"You live in number 2?"

"Yes."

The woman's expression changed. A flash of concern? Was it fear? Heather wasn't entirely sure. Whatever the woman's thoughts were they brought on the first sign of life and recognition to her otherwise deaden face. It was unnerving.

"You pregnant?"

"Yes, how…"

"You keep holding your belly."

"Oh."

"Look…" the woman bit her top lip. "You come and see me…if you need to."

"Okay," said Heather, frowning.

"If you need to…"

"I will…"

The woman closed the door in her face.

***

She walked up the rise to Mr Singh's shop, turning the conversation with the woman over in her mind. She assumed the woman was Rafferty's mother, but the boy held no resemblance to her. It wasn't just their features that differentiated them, it was their nature. Rafferty was a seemingly bright and happy child, friendly and talkative, his mother, if that was indeed his mother, was quite the opposite.

The woman had troubled Heather, particularly her cryptic message.

Come and see me…if you need to.

What had that meant? Heather turned it over in her mind, but deep down—down where she dared not look—she knew what the woman was referring to.

She was talking about the thing that haunted her house. Once Heather fixed on that, she couldn't shake it. That was exactly what the woman was talking about.

Come and see me…if you need to.

***

"Ah, Miss Heather Lowes," said Amar Singh, with a big smile on his face.

"Hello, Your Lordship."

He laughed. "Very good. You settled into the house?"

"Getting there," she said. She picked up milk and bread and a box of eggs and carried them over to the counter.

"It always takes a bit of time to get settled into somewhere new," he said. "And with a little one on the way, I see."

She looked down at her belly. She was holding it again. "Yes, it seems I'm getting all of life's major events ticked off in one year—new house, baby, and…" She trailed off.

"Yes, I am sorry to hear about your husband. Very sad."

"Someone told you?"

"When you run a shop Mrs Lowes, you hear everything."

"I see."

He began to add up the items.

Heather said, "What else have you heard?"

"I'm sorry?"

"About my house." She just blurted it out. She could hardly believe herself.

Amar looked at her. He put the milk down and said, "One pound ten, please."

She handed a pound note over and then rummaged about in her purse for the ten pence. She only had it in shrapnel and counted up ones and a few half pennies until she had the full amount. She felt foolish for asking him about her house and decided not to press the issue. If he didn't want to answer, then that was fine. She handed over the money and he put it in his till and closed it. Then he placed her items in a thin plastic bag. He handed the bag over to her. She felt something had shifted between them.

"Thank you," she said, and turned to go.

Amar Singh spoke: "Houses hold memories, Heather Lowes. And they have long memories. But the thing to remember is…they are just that. They are shadows. Echoes. They are not really there."

Heather looked at the shop keeper. She sensed that he wanted to say more, but didn't. He simply smiled brightly, as if what he'd just said hadn't happened, and then said, "Good evening, Heather Lowes. Be well."

"Thank you, Mr Singh."

"Please, Amar."

"Thank you, Amar."

"Very good, Heather. Come again soon."

***

She stood on the rise, looking down the hill towards Society Place. She picked out her rooftop, grey slates in the evening sun. She wondered about that little house. A little house at the end of a normal street in Derby. A little house that was now hers. Was it a notorious house? It certainly seemed to have a reputation. People seemed to know something, something they weren't telling her. This thought gave way to anger. Why weren't they telling her? If there was something wrong with the house, if something bad had happened there, why were people keeping it from her?

She started to walk back down the hill. The sun was low, bathing everything in an orange haze. The streets were quiet, very few cars, no kids out. Heather pushed dark thoughts from her mind and tried to focus on the present, on the beauty of the summer evening.

She approached the school. The bleak Victorian block of brick and glass. She noticed an archway at the bottom of the sheer frontage of the building, at street level. It was a large opening, blocked off by wire mesh. She crossed the road to take a closer look. The arch seemed to run down below the surface of the pavement. She came to it and touched the wire mesh, then cupped one hand around one eye to block out the light and peered into the gloom. The school appeared to be built on pillars, and between the ground and the underside of the building was a concreted area. It was difficult to see with any real clarity as it was so dark under there but it didn't seem to Heather that there was much of anything down there. It looked empty. She could make out a fence of some kind at the other end of the building, leading out to the playground beyond, but little else.

Heather wrinkled her nose. It smelt down there, smelt of damp and piss and God knows what else. It seemed a strange design for a school, particularly an old school like St Chad's. If Heather was to hazard a guess, she'd say the school had been built at the turn of the century, perhaps earlier. She crossed the plastic bag from one hand to the other as it was cutting into her fingers, the milk weighing it down considerably.

She moved to go when she thought she caught sight of something move in the dark beneath the school. A quick movement. The movement of someone slipping deeper into the darkness. It made her stomach lurch and her heart race.

She put the bag on the ground then stepped closer, pressing her face against the wire. She cupped both hands around her face and blinked her eyes until they adjusted to the dark. The movement had come from one of the pillars. They were large enough to easily hide behind and Heather felt sure there was somebody there. And that someone—or something—was listening, waiting for her to leave.

A car came up the rise and Heather looked around to see if they'd noticed her stood there, peering into the space beneath the school. They had. It was an old bloke and he stared straight at Heather, and continued to stare as he drove past. Once he was gone, she turned her head back to the dark and—

Something hit the wire. It made a loud thud and rattled the mesh. It caused Heather to yelp and leap back. She almost fell over her bag, but managed to steady herself. She stood on the box of eggs however, crushing them all.

She bent over, hands on her knees, trying to catch her breath. Then the pain came. A sudden lance in her stomach; a furious stabbing that caused her to double over even more. She cried out then gritted her teeth against the assault.

Something was very wrong.

CHAPTER NINE

Heather and Tony met at Clouds during one of Michael's gigs. Clouds was the epicentre for live acts in the mid-seventies. Heather had been many times in the days before she met Tony. She'd seen the likes of Uriah Heap, The Groundhogs, Chicken Shack, Status Quo, and many others there. It was a seedy little place; dark, grubby, loud, and was always packed to the rafters. Everyone she knew went there, and Michael's band, Candlestick Park, played often, sometimes supporting whatever big name was passing through on a given night. She'd seen Candlestick Park support the Edgar Broughton Band, Van der Graaf Generator and Caravan, among others. They blew Caravan away, in Heather's humble opinion.

On the night Heather met Tony, Candlestick Park were headlining, after being supported by another local covers band, Velvet Blend. Both bands going down a storm. Heather had got a little drunk and danced with her friend, Michelle. It was a Thursday night and she felt fantastic. She felt right in the moment; all she'd ever need was right there—friends, music, drink, and men.

And there were many men watching her dance. She knew it and on that particular night, she liked the attention. She'd returned a few smiles but hadn't acted on anything.

Until.

Candlestick Park were blasting through *John, I'm Only Dancing* when this one bloke walked in that caught Heather's eye right away. He was with a couple of mates and had long dark hair, a beard, and John Lennon glasses. He was tall, lean, and had a beautiful smile.

She took Michelle's hand and went to the bar. The place was rammed, as usual, so the girl's had to wait to get served. Tony had noticed the girls, and moved out the way to allow them to get to the bar, and that was pretty much it. They got talking right away, the connection immediate. By the time Candlestick Park got to their last song—Sabbath's *Sweat Leaf*—Michelle had drifted off, as had Tony's mates, leaving them huddled in a corner, shouting into each other's ears, getting closer and closer.

After Candlestick Park came off, the club continued playing music just as loud as the band's themselves. Michael came over to see if Heather was alright—gauging the situation, weighing Tony up—and then went off to talk to a blonde in fishnet stockings and a black PVC dress.

They danced to Wishbone Ash and 10CC and drank a little more and made each other laugh and learnt a little about one another and both felt that there was something different going on than a usual hook up in a club.

At kicking out time, everyone fell out onto the street and Tony met Michael properly and even helped the band (minus the singer) load the gear up into the back of the van. After that Michael drove off with the PVC blonde, leaving the rhythm section, Bill and The Stiff, to saunter off to get the bus.

Tony walked her across town to the house she shared with Michelle and another girl, Lucy, and he kissed her on the front step. It had felt like a real kiss, a deep kiss, a kiss that could lead to a life together.

They saw each other the very next night, and the night after that. On the fifth night they went to see *Tommy* at the ABC and then had sex in the backseat of Tony's yellow Hillman Avenger. After that they were never apart.

They'd met in June, 1975. By February of the following year, they were married.

By May, Tony was dead. He died in the Hillman Avenger.

***

Evelyn Green was worried about the woman next door. She'd been getting ready for bed when she saw the ambulance lights and heard voices and commotion coming from her house. However, by the time she'd put on her dressing gown over her nightie and had gotten downstairs and to the front door, the ambulance was just turning out of Society Place and heading up the rise.

Night was coming on, but there was still light in the sky. It was also hot still but that had been a constant since May. She got into bed but couldn't sleep. The curtains were drawn, the room was dark, but still she lay there. She thought about reading a little—she had a Mills & Boon by her bed—but she decided to just try and close her eyes. She lay still for all of thirty seconds before turning over, kicking the covers from her. Her mind raced. She couldn't stop thinking about the lovely young woman next door and hoped to God she was alright. She felt awful for that woman—a widow so young, and a mother-to-be, alone, in that house. It had been a constant worry for Evelyn ever since she'd met Heather Lowes properly over the weekend. Such a nice girl, pretty and sweat, and so full of hurt. Of all the houses, why did such a lovely and fragile girl have to move into that house?

She turned over again. She was hot and clammy. She thought about the house. It had been quiet for so long, but with the young woman's arrival, something had reawakened. Evelyn could feel it. She'd felt it before, an uneasy feeling emanating from the walls that divided her house and that house. She looked at the wall now across from her. A chest-of-drawers stood up against it, John Constable's *The Hay Wain* on the wall. She could feel it now, or so she imagined. Perhaps that was why she hadn't been sleeping well, that or the heat. It was more than likely the heat—at her age, the summer had just been too much for Evelyn—but still, that house had certainly caused her concern again.

She turned over again and sighed. A car went by on the road below her window. She thought about getting up and going back downstairs. Perhaps doing some knitting to help calm her, but decided against. She had to get some sleep.

She closed her eyes and tried to lie as still as possible. She thought about her husband, Albert, as often she did last thing at night. She thought about how they were when they were young, how handsome he was, how full of life he'd been—how full of life she'd been. It all seemed like a very long time ago, and yet, it didn't. It seemed long ago in years, but not in memory.

Thinking of Albert and of being young, the trips they'd taken to Blackpool, the Christmases they'd had when Matthew was a boy, soothed her. Her house had seen so much. So much life and laughter and happiness and also so much sadness and loneliness. The loneliness far worse to bear than the sadness because, often, the sadness is bittersweet, it can ebb and flow, whereas loneliness is permanent: an ever present spectre that can gnaw away at you. She turned over again, but settled into thinking about Albert again.

She was finally drifting off, when a sound caused her to sit bolt upright and stare at the wall across from her. The sound had been that of a scratching, of that she was sure. A scratching coming from the other side of the wall.

She stared, wide-eyed, her breathing heavy. She stared at the chest-of-drawers and the Constable painting of three horses pulling a cart through a river. She listened hard.

There was nothing for a long time then it came again. A scratching, fingernails at the wall. Evelyn tried to pinpoint its location and looked just right of the Constable, high up in the corner. It stopped then scratched again, this time in a different area of the wall, now bottom left, past the legs of the chest-of-drawers. Then it stopped and nothing happened for a long time. Long enough for her breathing to steady and her heart to slow.

A loud thud came. Evelyn screamed, her heart racing.

Then another thud. The sound of a fist thumping the wall. At least, that's what it sounded like to Evelyn.

Another thud. And another, and another, until Evelyn was practically having palpitations. She couldn't catch her breath.

Thud, Thud, Thud.

Over and over again.

Its rhythm got faster and harder.

THUD THUD THUD.

Evelyn fell out of bed. She was crying now, holding her chest, shaking uncontrollably.

THUD THUD THUD.

The Constable fell from the wall and smashed down on the chest-of-drawers. Evelyn was screaming. Anger gave way to fear and she managed to find her voice:

"STOP IT!!" she screamed, and just like that, the banging stopped.

Stopped dead, giving way to sudden silence.

Evelyn whimpered and lay back on the floor, panting.

She knew now for certain that the thing that haunted number 2, Society Place was back.

She knew she had to tell Heather Lowes everything.

CHAPTER TEN

Michael arrived at the hospital just after eleven. He'd got in from rehearsals around half ten and found his phone ringing. It was Heather. She told him where she was and told him not to panic, everything was okay. The baby was fine, she was fine, but she needed him to come and get her. Half an hour later, Michael was at the Derby Royal Infirmary.

Heather was sat in a wheelchair when he saw her; she looked deathly pale. He rushed to her and she told him to stop fussing. She grabbed hold of his hand and stood up. They were in an ill-lit corridor by the natal ward. There were very few people about and Michael found the place eerie. He didn't like hospitals.

"They said I've got a urine infection," said Heather. "They've given me some antibiotics and it should be fine. Baby's okay, she's just been pressing down on my bladder that's all."

"She?"

"Yes, I think she's a girl."

"What makes you think that?"

She thought for a moment then said, "Mother's intuition."

"I see. So my niece has been playing about with your insides?"

"More like she's been squashing my bits, making it difficult to pee. It's just got a bit messy down there..."

Michael looked decidedly uncomfortable.

Heather laughed. "Don't look so freaked out. Look, Mum and Dad died on us so you've got to hear all this personal stuff now."

"Great," he said, rolling his eyes.

She looked at him. "Thank you for coming."

"Of course I'd come."

"You've been so good to me."

Michael noticed her eyes water. "Hey, hey," he said. "Let's get you home. This place gives me the creeps."

She wiped her eyes. "I forgot you hate hospitals."

They began to walk down the corridor.

"They're horrible places," he said. "Like great big tombstones."

***

Neither of them spoke much on the way back to Society Place, not at first. Michael had on his 8-track. It was Black Sabbath. *War Pigs* gave way to *Laguna Sunrise* and Heather rested her head against the glass and watched the night. She wished she and Michael could just go back home but their house belonged to another family now—strangers that lived within the walls they grew up in. She'd always felt so safe at home. Her father's embrace, her mother's apron, the back door open, the kettle whistling. Heather thought it would always be like that; a place of unmovable foundations, a nexus that would never corrupt, never change. She wondered how she could have ever thought of life being full of such certainties.

Death and taxes, the old joke went, they were the only certainties in life.

"Do you remember their faces?" Heather asked her brother.

"Who? Mum and Dad?"

"Yes."

He stopped at a red light, the engine idling. "Do you?" he said.

She looked ahead at the cars crossing the junction. "They're hazy," she said, finally. "They're just something from a half remembered dream. I have to really concentrate to fix them in my mind. Don't you think that's sad?"

"No...it's natural." The lights turned green and he pulled away.

"Is it?"

"Yeah. Look, it was a long time ago. Life moves on. We were given a shitty deal, but we got through it. That's what people do; they get through shit."

"I suppose," she said, then fell silent.

Laguna Sunrise finished and Michael reached over and turned off the 8-track. He took a right onto Silver Hill Road and changed down to second, then first as the van struggled up the hill.

All the houses were in darkness, save one or two with dim light behind drawn curtains. They turned into Society Place and Heather felt unease creep over her. She realised it had been there all night, the creep that is—all day, in fact—but it immediately intensified as they approached her house. She thought about what Amar Singh had said to her. *Houses holds memories*, he'd said, but that, *they are shadows. Echoes. They are not really there.*

How did he know about her house? She wondered if he knew *what* was in her house. Did everybody know? They seemed to.

As they pulled up outside number 2, Society Place, she decided to confront everybody, first thing in the morning, starting with Mrs Green.

Michael turned off the van and got out. She watched him pass the windscreen then he opened the passenger door and held her hand as she got out.

"Thank you for coming to get me."

"Shut up and get to bed."

She put the key in the lock and turned. She thought she heard something move inside the house then abruptly stop at the sound of the front door opening.

She flicked the light on and stepped into the front room, Michael right behind her.

Heather noticed right away that her chair had moved its position and was now in the centre of the room.

***

Michael went through to the kitchen and he ducked his head under the tap and drank cold water. The night air was stifling and he was parched. He wondered when the heat wave was going to break. Heather shuffled about behind him. He turned off the tap and wiped his mouth.

"Do you want a cup of tea?" she asked.

"No," he said, turning to her. "It's too hot for tea. I'll just see you to bed and then I'll be off."

"I'm not five, Michael."

"I know, but I'd feel better knowing you're safely tucked up."

She looked annoyed and a little distracted. Michael noticed she kept looking around the place. She also looked very tired.

"Bed," he said.

Heather looked at him, but didn't say anything then she crossed the kitchen to the stairway. She seemed to hover at the foot of the stairs, but finally leaned in and turned on the light. Michael pictured her as a little girl again, afraid to run across the dark landing they used to have.

"You okay?" he asked her.

She stood with her back to him. "Yes. Goodnight."

She ran up the stairs. He heard her enter the bedroom and slam the door shut. He raised his eyebrows and looked around. There was a notepad on the floor by the kitchen table, along with a few pens. He went over and picked these up. He noticed a shopping list on the pad in Heather's familiar neat handwriting. Below the list were two questions—*Who are you? What are you?*

Michael puzzled over the questions for a moment then noticed something else beneath the table. He crouched down and stared at a scattering of dead ladybirds. He flicked one to make sure it was dead. It bounced off the skirting and stopped against a chair leg, upturned. Many of the creatures were upturned. He looked around the kitchen floor and noticed more, mainly in corners and up against the units. There were a great number across the room.

He went back across the kitchen and rummaged about under the sink. He found a dustpan and brush and went about sweeping them all up. He heard Heather banging about in her room upstairs.

Once the ladybirds were all collected up in the dustpan he opened the back door and went down the yard to the bin. He tipped the dustpan into the rubbish and then looked back to the house. The little light from the stairway was spilling into the back room: a neat line of dark and light across the ceiling. Then the line moved, as if the door in the room was being pushed inwards. He figured Heather was going to the bathroom and he went back inside.

He locked the back door, put the dustpan and brush back under the sink, then went over to the stairway. He stood on the bottom step and called up. "Heather…"

Her door was shut, but he heard her moving about in there. She wasn't in the bathroom after all. "Heather," he called again.

"What?"

"You alright?"

"Yes." Her voice sounded strained.

"You sure?"

"Goodnight, Michael."

He hesitated then shook his head and left.

***

Heather heard Michael slam the front door. She turned off the bedroom light and then went over to the window, being careful not to trip over any of the clutter. She peered down into the street and saw Michael get into his van. He fired it up and she heard Sabbath burst into life—the opening roar of *Tomorrow's Dream*—and she watched as he slowly pulled away from the curb. He got to the end of the street, his indicator flashing right, up the rise, but he didn't move. The van idled, *Tomorrow's Dream* like a distant rumble.

She watched, wondering what he was doing, wondering if he was going to back up and return to the house but then he revved the engine and the van sputtered on up the rise.

Heather turned away from the window and looked at her room in the darkness. All the bed covers were across the floor, clothes had been ripped from hangers in the alcove, and her bedside table had been upturned, the small lamp broken on the carpet.

She placed her hands on her belly and tried to control her breathing.

She looked at her bedroom door and felt the presence out on the stairway.

CHAPTER ELEVEN

As he drove, Michael worried about Heather. Something was not right. Not right with her and not right with the house she lived in. Not right at all. He turned off the 8-track once *Sweet Leaf* had faded out.

The roads were quiet. He rolled his window down and enjoyed the night breeze on his skin. He thought about how his parents died.

***

Michael had been sixteen, and Heather, fourteen. It was Easter time, winter was fading away and the world seemed in bloom. Spring had always been Michael's favourite season. It was a reawakening from those drab, dark months. The promise of summer was ahead, and the world filled up with light again. Now he hated the season, as must Heather, he thought. A season haunted by not just her parents' death but also her husband's. Now it was the darkest season.

It had been a collision with a lorry on the A38, just outside of Somercotes, in the Amber Valley. They'd been coming back from a birthday party in Ripley, and were both in fancy dress. June, Michael and Heather's mother, had been dressed as Cleopatra, and their father, George, was the Man with No Name. He had given his best Clint Eastwood scowl as they left that night. "Look after your sister," he'd said, with Clint-style grit and gravel. It was the last thing he ever said to his son. Words that would eventually hold tremendous weight.

June, only thirty-three at the time, had looked fantastic as Cleopatra. Heather had told her she looked just like Liz Taylor and June had blushed. She had though. Her final words to her offspring had been, "Don't eat all the crisps in the cupboard." Very little weight could be placed on these words, but then, Michael surmised, most last words must be trivial. Unless you knew that the end is coming, no grand statement could be lifted from the banality of day to day conversation. *Look after your sister* however was a different matter. It was a line George Grant had said to his son a thousand times over the course of Michael's young life, said in causal caution, but after that night it become a code of honour on how Michael had to live his life. He always did look out for Heather, and always would.

They'd headed home after the birthday party around half eleven. Both had been drinking, but George had said he felt fine and they headed back to Derby on the dark bypass of the A38. The lorry had been coming off the slip road onto the bypass. Either George had been driving too fast, or he just didn't notice it, but he left it too late to swerve and went right into the back of the lorry. The front of the car crushed up like an aluminium can and then span across lanes and smashed into the central reservation. June went through the windscreen and was struck by a car heading in the opposite direction.

George, on the other hand, was crushed against his steering wheel, but didn't die instantly. He remained alive for a good fifteen minutes or more, sitting there, looking out at the night, seeing the smear of his wife on the tarmac across from him, wondering who would tell his children that both their parents were dead. For he knew he was going to die.

The lorry driver stayed with him until the ambulance came but George Grant died looking at the flashing blue lights, dressed as Clint Eastwood, never even getting to glimpse the paramedics that came rushing towards him.

Heather had gone to bed around nine o'clock and Michael had taken advantage of his night of freedom and stayed up until eleven watching *Budgie* with Adam Faith. Both were asleep when the police knocked on their door at four in the morning.

***

Michael pulled up outside his flat and turned the engine off. He sat in the quiet for a long while, listening to the night, smelling the summer air. He began to cry.

CHAPTER TWELVE

Evelyn Green was making toast with jam when there was a knock at the front door. She knew who it was before she answered it.

It was time.

She let Heather in and began to make a pot of tea. The back door was open and there was birdsong and the sound of children playing out on the street. Heather sat at her kitchen table. She didn't say a word. She looked pale and tired.

Evelyn discarded her toast and jam and got out cups and saucers from her glass cabinet. She placed one before Heather, who gave a thin smile of thanks, then put the other cup and saucer on her side. The kettle whistled and she got her oven-glove and poured the hot water into the pot and put the lid back on.

All through these mundane tasks, Evelyn could feel the fear and confusion emanating from the young woman sat at her kitchen table.

Still wearing the oven-glove, Evelyn carried the pot over to the table and placed it down on a mat. She took off the glove then sat down across from Heather Lowes.

Evelyn looked at her, but Heather kept her eyes lowered.

Evelyn listened to the sound of a jet plane overhead, and the children squealing and laughing out on the street. A dog was barking. A distant radio was playing. Evelyn's clock was ticking.

She poured the tea, stirred in the milk—a spoon against china, a comforting sound—and then leaned back in her chair. It creaked.

"Is your baby alright?" she asked.

Heather answered without looking up. "Yes."

"Good."

"Are you alright?"

Heather didn't answer.

The sound of the plane faded away.

Heather looked at her at last and Evelyn didn't like her dark eyes, her tired, frightened eyes. She'd seen those eyes before.

Finally, Heather spoke, barely above a whisper: "What is in my house?"

Although Evelyn knew the question was coming it still caused her spine to react and the hairs on her arms to stand up in attention of fear.

"I'm not going to lie to you, my dear," she said. "You need to know, for you and your baby's sake."

"My baby?"

"Yes."

"It's bad, isn't it?"

"Yes."

"Is it dangerous?"

"I think so."

"Has it always been there?"

"No. It was invited."

"Invited?"

"Conjured, I suppose you could say."

Heather frowned. She looked angry, lost, fragile.

"Do you know what it is?"

"No. I've only heard it...through the walls."

"Mrs Green, did you know my house was haunted when I moved in?"

"Yes." She looked guilty. "But...I thought it had gone away. It had been quiet for so long."

"Gone away?"

"I thought it went away when Shaw left."

"Who the hell is Shaw?"

"The man who lived in your house."

***

Michael had got to his sister's early. He'd found her already up and dressed. She hadn't looked good. She said she was going next door to Mrs Green's, which was a relief to Michael as he didn't want her to see him carrying all the bricks and mortar down to the cellar.

He waited until she'd gone before he unloaded the van. It took several trips to get all the bricks, the tools, the shovel, and the bags of sand and cement down there but he did it fast in case Heather came back. Once everything was down there, he locked his van up then gave himself a moment to look at the beautiful clear blue sky. Kids were already out on the street and he felt a pang of nostalgia fill his heart. To be that age again, he thought.

He went back inside.

He filled a bucket from the sink in the kitchen then went down to begin work (making sure he firmly closed the cellar door behind him). He unscrewed the piece of boarding and laid it down to use as a spot board. A rush of cold air emanated from the hole. He mixed the sand and cement with the shovel. He turned the mortar over and over until it was just right for laying then he rifled through his tool bag for his trowel. The cold air was still coming from the hole. There was a stink to it also, like a smell of rotting eggs. He gave the gear another quick turn with the trowel then stood up, looking at the hole.

He rubbed his beard and sighed, his nose offended by the cold stink.

He went back up to van to get a torch.

***

"Shaw moved into the house in 1963," said Evelyn Green. "I remember because it was a dreadful winter that year. Snow up to the knees. A nice family lived in the house before that—all through the fifties. The Rogers. They had two sons who used to play with Matthew. Then Shaw moved in." Her eyes darkened.

"I never saw him for the first few weeks. No one did. He drew all the curtains and never came out. But I'd hear things..."

"Like what?"

"Like...chanting."

"Chanting?"

"Yes. A continual murmur that would go on and on, round and round, day and night."

"What was he saying?"

"I could never decipher it. After about a week of it I started banging on the walls and, at first, it did the trick. Then, one bitterly cold day, there was a knock at my door."

Heather looked past Mrs Green to the front door in the next room. She caught sight of a ladybird fluttering in the gap between the kitchen and the front room, by the door of Mrs Green's cellar. She turned her attention back to her host. "Shaw?" she asked.

"Yes. I was surprised to see he was just a boy, perhaps a little younger than yourself—twenty maybe, twenty-one—a spring chicken, as we used to say. Anyway, he looked dreadful. Terribly thin, gaunt, looked like he hadn't eaten in weeks. His hair was long as well...and greasy looking. This was before those Beatles came along with their mop tops, before I'd heard anything about them anyways, and the length of that boy's hair was quite something to behold in 1963. Nowadays all the young 'uns have long hair, but back then it was short back and sides, make no mistake.

"Any road, he's out there in the snow in nothing but a pair of pyjamas and black boots. He unnerved me right away. I had the door on the latch and I peered out at him. He looked at me, but didn't speak, not at first. In fact he didn't seem to be focusing on me at all. It was like he was looking through me. A thousand yard stare, I think they call it. Also, he seemed to be swaying, like he was about to keel over. I'll never forget it. Then he said to me, 'You got any coal. I'm freezing to death,' just like that. No hello or excuse me or anything. But you see, I was so unnerved by that point, his rudeness didn't even register until later."

"What did you do?"

"I got my coat on and went down the yard and opened the gate so he could help himself to my coal. What could I have done? There was a shed at the end back then. I had it torn down a few years back; it was falling to bits. He never thanked me, but I saw him coming and going for a good hour or more, loading up one bucket after another. He had a strange, jerky movement to him. He put me in mind of a bird. One of those ugly overgrown things. Like an ostrich or one of those emus I've seen on the telly. He was so long and thin. You know the other funny thing? He collected up the coal still dressed in his pyjamas. No wonder he said he was freezing to death, trudging through the snow in nowt but threads. There were no fat on him…just skin and bone he were."

Heather was getting impatient, but didn't want to push the old lady in case she clammed up on her. Then, without any further prompting, Mrs Green said something that quite astonished Heather.

"My dear…do you believe in magic?"

***

Michael shone the torch down the hole. The torch wasn't great and the light only went so far before it was swallowed by darkness. It certainly went through to next door's cellar, maybe even further. Michael realised that Paul might've been right after all: the tunnel could well run the length of the entire street.

Michael reached in and ran his fingers over the brickwork. The bricks themselves were very old, mortar and redbrick dust coming away in his hand. It looked dangerous. The smell was stronger now he had his head poking down the hole. It did remind him of rancid eggs, and he figured something had crawled down there and died. A cat maybe or a rodent of some kind. He pulled his t-shirt up over his nose and got down on his knees and ventured a little deeper into the mouth of the tunnel.

***

"I'm talking about true magic," said the old woman. "Not the Abracadabra, variety show magic. Real magic…"

Heather considered this for a moment then said, "Yes, I believe I do."

"Good," said Evelyn Green, a glint of mischief in her eyes. "When I was a little girl, I believed there were fairies at the bottom of the garden. I believed my grandmother was a witch. A good witch, I must add. She could *do* things…see things. She knew when things were going to happen. She could predict them. Small things, a change in the weather, a door about to be knocked on, and by whom. Most would put these things down to mere coincidence, but she did them too often to be put down to such simple explanation. She could bend providence to her will. I also saw her put hexes on people. I remember my Uncle Sid wronging my grandfather somehow and my old grandmother stood and pointed at him with crooked fingers—a magical shape—and she kicked him out of the house. The next day he fell off a ladder and broke his leg. I was a little girl then, but I knew what she was.

"Through her I learned there was good magic and there was bad magic, dark magic. Black magic. What that young man did in your house in the few years he lived there was the darkest magic. Unholy magic. Magic used to summon the dead."

Heather saw more ladybirds fluttering around Mrs Green's cellar door.

***

Michael was on all fours, his torch between his teeth. He was sweating, despite the cold in the tunnel. He decided he'd gone far enough; he was never going to see anything other than darkness, so began to back up, but something caused him to stop. A noise from deep in the dark. It was faint, but it was there: a scratching sound, fingernails on brick.

He took the torch from his mouth and listened. He was breathing heavy, his heart thumped against his chest.

He held the torch out in front of him and probed the dark but he saw nothing. Moreover, the sound had stopped, and he immediately began to wonder whether he'd heard anything in the first place. He continued to listen, then shook his head and backed up again. But then a charge of fear shot down his spine.

He felt a presence behind him.

***

"So what are you telling me?" said Heather. "Some deranged kid performed occult ceremonies over a decade ago and raised some sort of spirit that lingers still to this day?"

Evelyn Green looked at the young woman. She understood her denial, her anger, her confusion. She understood that Heather probably thought she was being taken for a ride, that she was being hoodwinked, conned, teased with a fanciful story of ghosts and dark magicians. Who would believe such a thing? She also realised that the girl had suffered immense loss and the last thing she needed to hear was that her house was haunted.

But she needed to know.

Evelyn spoke softly and said, "Yes, Heather, there is something in your house that must be removed."

"Removed?"

"Yes."

"I suppose you're suggesting I get a priest and have an exorcism?" Her voice was rising.

"Perhaps."

"Look, this is insane." Heather stood up. "I can see and touch this." She slammed her palm down on the table. "It's real. I'm real, you're real. I can hear the kids playing out on the street and there's a plane going by. This is normality. This is real. This is the world. People may think they see all sorts of things, but there's no hard scientific evidence to prove any of it. They've never come up with a single shred of evidence to suggest there's anything supernatural. We live, we die, that's it."

Evelyn let her have her moment then very calmly, she said. "I understand your anger, Heather. I do. It's not easy to accept, but there is more to life than this. Yes, the kettle boils, the children play, people go to and from work. Ordinary lives go about their days, but hidden from most eyes are things beyond our understanding. This is a haunted country, of that there is no doubt, whether scientists can see it or not. I've seen it and always have, right from girlhood, when my grandmother taught me how to open my eyes to such things. She had many names for ghosts. Some of them used to make me laugh—scrags, fetches, mum-pokers, spoorns, freits, ouphs, hobs, all kinds of names, she had—but they were never funny when I saw them. Even my husband…"

"You saw your husband?" Heather sat back down.

"Yes," said Evelyn. "He was a dear man and he came to me tenderly, but I was still fearful of him and I hid my face from him. I feel such guilt about that. I wish I could have held my gaze and accepted his apparition, his hob, but I could not.

"But think on this Heather Lowes…to believe in the supernatural is to open your eyes to it, to accept it as a truth, and in that there is hope, optimism…there is light."

"Light?" said Heather. "How so?"

"Because to see a ghost is to tell us that there is life beyond death. That there is such a thing as a soul, and that we continue beyond this mere flesh and bone. Is that not hopeful?"

Heather didn't say anything at first. She looked past Mrs Green to the gathering of ladybirds that were now crawling over the cellar door.

"But the thing in my house…that is not full of light?"

Mrs Green's eyes darkened. "No…no it is not."

"What can I do?"

"I believe you have to strip that house back to the brick and clean its walls. Cleanse it of its dark past."

Heather looked back to the cellar door. The ladybirds were gone.

***

Beads of sweats dripped from Michael's brow. He couldn't move. He felt the presence behind him, perhaps staring down the hole at him. He felt its hunger, its wildness. He couldn't rationalise these senses, they just came to him. Whatever was behind him was malevolent, of that he was certain. He felt the darkness.

He remained still. There, in a hole, on all fours. Trapped by whatever was stood at the opening behind him. He listened. He waited. He closed his eyes and tried to make sense of his thoughts but they were a tangled mess. He realised he was feeling true fear, a deep permeating dread that rattled through him. A fear the likes of which he hadn't felt since the night his parents died.

He swallowed and opened his eyes. He said, "That's enough," and just like that the thing was gone. He felt it with certainty.

He scrambled backwards and fell out of the hole, his right shoulder landing in the mortar he'd just mixed.

He sat up and wiped the muck away. He composed himself, then picked up his trowel and began to run the first course of bricks in. He was no bricklayer, and it was a shoddy job, but it didn't need to look good. The hole just needed to be filled.

He sang while he worked. He sang *All Along the Watchtower* very loudly.

CHAPTER THIRTEEN

Rafferty was trying to watch *Rentaghost*, a show he normally loved but for some reason he couldn't get into it. He felt distracted, ill at ease. His arm was in plaster and in a sling to boot plus his ribs still hurt as did the various cuts and bruises up and down his body. He'd been having trouble sleeping; he just couldn't get comfortable plus, he'd been having bad dreams. Very bad dreams.

His mother was in the kitchen, clattering about, humming a tune that was distracting and annoying in itself. He knew the song—*Let 'Em In* by Wings—and his mum had a nice voice, but still, it was annoying while he was trying to watch the box.

He sat stewing on the sofa. Raff liked the jester ghost best and he normally had him rolling about laughing, but not today. Today Raff was sick of the heat, sick of his itchy arm, sick of the cuts and bruises, sick of his street, his house, his mum singing; he was sick of *Rentaghost* and he was sick of his mates outside kicking a ball about. He wanted the summer to end, yet he didn't want to go back to school. He wanted his arm to get better but he didn't want to play on the street. He didn't want to see anyone. He wanted to sleep, and not have the bad dreams. He wanted to leave Society Place and never come back.

He'd thought about running away, but knew he would never do it. He was fearful of his father but he loved his mother, even if everyone else found her a bit strange. His friends teased him about her all the time. They called her a nutter and said other mean things, but Raff gave as good as he got. Insulting each other's mothers was just the way of things.

There was a knock on the front window and Rafferty looked up to see several of his mates peering in. "You coming out, Raff," he heard one of them say. "Come on!"

Raff's mother came through to see what all the noise was.

"Why don't you go out?" she said to him.

"I don't want to."

His mates were still knocking on the window and calling his name.

"It's a lovely day, Raff, and you've not been out for ages. It'll do you good."

"No," he said.

"Err, I don't want that attitude, thank you very much."

She went over to the window and shouted, "He's still ill," and shooed them all away. Raff watched them go running off down the street. His mother came and stood over him.

"Look, you're back at school next week, so I suggest you get up tomorrow morning and go out and make the most of it. I can't have you sitting around the house all day; I've got things to do."

Rentaghost finished and Raff got up and turned the TV off.

"Are you listening to me?"

"Yes."

He went through to the kitchen and his mother called after him. "Where you going now? I'm talking to you?"

"To my room," he said and raced up the stairs before she could say anymore.

***

In his room, Rafferty sat up on his toy chest by the window and stared out at the big tree. It looked peaceful out there in the sunshine, its branches rich green and sprawling across fence tops and garden sheds. It didn't look like a tree that could cut and scrape and bruise, it didn't look like it could split lips, crack ribs, and break bones. It looked like a sleeping giant.

Raff scanned the surrounding backyards. A few doors down, Lee Cope's little brother was laughing and banging, playing about with some toy Raff couldn't quite see. Mr Newbold was in his greenhouse, pottering about, and next door to him, Mrs Lang was hanging out her washing. Raff turned his head and glimpsed, over Mrs Green's wall, the young woman, Heather, stood in her yard. He pressed his face up against the glass, straining to see her and was then disturbed to find that she was crying.

He couldn't hear her, but he could see her, and she was really sobbing. Seeing any grown-up cry was upsetting, but this was more than upsetting, this was unsettling. Rafferty thought about the thing in her house and got really scared. He ran to his bed and threw the cover back with his one good arm. He got in and winced as he adjusted his position to allow for his sling then he pulled the covers over his head. It was safe under there, nothing could get him. He thought about going to see Mrs Lowes, but dismissed the idea right away. The thought of going anywhere near that house filled him with a terrible dread.

He kicked the covers down and lay there. Sunlight streamed into his room. He could hear his friends playing out on the front, his mother banging about in the kitchen below him. All appeared to be normal, except it wasn't. None of it was normal because it was all tainted. Tainted by whatever lay inside Mrs Lowes' house and perhaps inside his own house. It tainted the sun, his friend's laughter, the safety of his room; it tainted the backyards, the tree, the jitty, everything. All of it, tainted by darkness.

He got up and forced himself to go back to the window. He pressed up against the glass and strained to see, but Mrs Lowes was gone. Her yard empty.

She must have gone back inside the house.

That house.

CHAPTER FOURTEEN

Michael had managed to tune in ITV so Heather spent the evening watching telly: *Crossroads*, followed by *The Bionic Woman*, followed by *The Benny Hill Show*, one after the other. She sat and stared at the screen, not really taking in what was happening. Only *The Bionic Woman* caught her attention a little as she idly wished she was Lindsay Wagner, with all that power, and, moreover, wished she was also in California, far away from Society Place, and her grief, and her ghost.

It was Thursday night. Tomorrow she would start her new job at Presto's as a till girl. Normally she would have embraced a new job, a new challenge, new people, but with everything that was going on, she was just dreading it. Still, it would get her out of the house.

The previous two nights had been quiet. Michael had been there much of the time, working down in the cellar. He hadn't allowed her down there; he'd said that the paint fumes wouldn't be good for the baby, so she stayed away. She busied herself with household chores and preparing her and Michael an evening meal. She'd even taken time to relax—much to Michael's urging—and sat in the yard on a deck chair and read a book in the sun—Peter Benchley's *The Deep*, which she'd got from the library and was thoroughly enjoying. It was pure escapism.

She also went to see her midwife, just to make sure everything was okay. The midwife, a plump, middle-aged woman with a nice face, had been chatty and friendly while she felt Heather's stomach. She assured Heather that everything was fine and urged her to relax. *Sit out in the sun*, she'd said. *Get a tan*.

When Heather got home that afternoon, Michael allowed her to see what he'd done in the cellar. He told her to cover her mouth, so she pulled her t-shirt up to her nose. Michael had painted the entire room white. It looked a little thrown on in places but it did look and smell clean.

She made a shepherd's pie for them both and they ate in relative silence. He helped wash up and then went home and the house closed in on her once more.

***

Benny Hill was chasing several young girls around in their underwear: the film speeded up, the canned laughter hysterical. Heather got up and turned off the telly then she went through to the kitchen and sat on the back step and looked to the bruised sky, the first stars glimmering in the dying day. She noticed a ladybird crawl on her arm and she flicked it away. She felt the stairway behind her.

She thought about Michael, about how quiet he'd been. She suspected he was just getting annoyed of constantly having to look after his little sister—his hopeless, grieving, pregnant sister. No wonder he was annoyed. He was probably worried that she wouldn't be able to cope with the baby and he'd have to become more than an uncle. He was in his mid-twenties, played guitar in a rock band, and had girls throwing themselves at him. The last thing he'd want was to become some sort of a surrogate father to the girl. He'd been wonderful to her since Tony's death but eventually he'd grow tired and step away. He was bound to, and she couldn't blame him for that. This was her mess, not his, and she was going to have to make the best of it.

She stood up and closed the back door. The house was quiet. She looked across the kitchen to the opening of the stairway. It was dark. She could feel *its* presence waiting for her.

"Listen," she said, her voice shaky to her ears. "We're going to have to lay down some ground rules…"

Silence. She felt stupid, but licked her lips and carried on.

"Look, I am not this person. I'm not this fragile little girl. That's not who I am. Admittedly you haven't caught me at my best moment but my husband of four months upped and died on me and then I found out I was with child, so it's kinda knocked me for six, if you know what I mean. Plus, this house is taking some getting used to, and you're not exactly helping…"

The more she spoke, the more confident she felt.

"…I was never like this. I used to have fun, be full of optimism and hope, but death royally dragged that out of me. First my parents, when I was younger…then my husband—all of them taken in car crashes. Imagine that. I mean, what are the chances? I don't think I'll ever learn to drive. Is that some kind of providence or what? Some kind of cosmic joke? Come on, you're dead, tell me…" She laughed. "Someone out there fucking with me or something?"

She let the question hang. No reply came.

"And who are you anyway? Were you *summoned* here by that kid? What was he doing down in my cellar? Tell me?"

Her voice was rising and it felt good.

"Well I'll tell you what, you can stay if you want, but make no mistake, this is *my* house now. Got it?"

Nothing.

"Just stay out of my way. I've got enough to deal with."

She walked across the kitchen, anger fuelling her adrenaline. When she got to the opening she put a hand to her belly. She flicked on the light, took one step, two steps, three. Then she stopped.

In a sudden, revolting wave there came the smell of rotting eggs. She gagged but then froze.

The thing was behind her.

At her back.

At her neck.

She held her belly.

The only thing she could hear was the blood thumping in her head. In her peripheral vision she saw her right hand gripping the banister and her left flat on the wall. She was splayed. Like a sacrifice.

Her breath caught. It was not *her* hand on her belly.

She looked down.

There was a man's hand on her. Dirty, slimy, with black fingernails and hair on the knuckles.

It dug its fingers into her.

She couldn't move, couldn't breathe, couldn't think. There was a dead man at her back, kneading her belly, his stench rancid.

The thing on her stairs had come to say hello and Heather was ill prepared for their meeting. It may have once been a man, but now it was a thing most foul.

She felt her bladder give way and it ran from her shorts, down her legs, to the carpeted stairs, but she still couldn't move. The hand kneaded her roughly, hurting her, and then she thought of her baby—a thought that refocused her mind and reawakened her senses.

She screamed out and the thing let go of her, but it didn't back away completely. She sensed it rise up, feet leaving the cheap carpet.

Heather brought both hands to her belly and began to whimper. She dared not turn around. She couldn't bring herself to look upon its face. It was enough that it floated behind her.

Her hands still clutching her belly, she squeezed her eyes shut and lifted one foot, very slowly, onto the next step. She sensed the thing moving about behind her. She took the step, then slowly brought her other leg up to the step beyond that and ascended once more.

It floated up the stairs with her. Every step taken, it remained at her back, hovering, emanating its stench, eyes boring into the back of her head. Her bedroom door was closed. The spare room door was closed. The top of the landing looked very far away, but still she climbed.

She heard scraping. It was running its dirty nails along the walls. It was taunting her, tormenting her, fucking with her. A wave of anger rattled through her and she took the last few steps in quick succession.

Then she was outside her door. At that moment, the fear gripped her stronger than ever before. She thought her legs were going to give way, but she somehow remained rigid. Still she did not turn around. She felt *it* above her, looking down at her, its fingers still scraping the walls, the ceiling, tapping, scratching, knocking, playing.

She took one hand from her belly and placed it on her door handle.

Then…

Then she began to sing. She sang *Silly Love Songs* and the tapping, the scratching, it all stopped. It still hovered above her, but she felt the change in its emotion. Its sense of play was gone. She felt its anger, its rage.

She sang louder and turned the door handle.

The thing floated down. She felt it at her neck.

She stopped singing and closed her eyes. She saw her husband and his image gave her strength. She said, "That's enough. Go away."

It did not go away.

Her hand still on the handle, she pushed the door, but only ajar, just enough.

"Go away," she said.

It did not.

Then she screamed "GO!"

She rushed into the room, feeling the thing rush towards her. She slammed the door on it and there was a thump against the wood. Then the thing began to bang on the door, again and again and again. So loud, with such fury.

Heather screamed, backing away from the door.

"GO AWAY...GO AWAY...GO!"

The banging stopped.

Heather held her breath. Her hands returned to their protective place upon her stomach.

The weight of thing was gone, its stench, gone. Heather fell back on the bed, panting.

Outside her window, the last of the day's light lingered in the night sky. Stars glistened; a crescent moon was riding high. A car rolled by on the road below. Out in the world, the steady rhythm of life continued on, but within her house of bricks, Heather knew now, without question, she was living with the dead.

PART TWO
1976/2019

CHAPTER FIFTEEN

Poppy hired a car at the airport. It took some adjusting having to drive on the other side of the road again, but she managed to make it out onto the motorway without incident. She stayed in the crawler lane for the first ten miles or so. Her plane had landed at 4a.m., and now, heading east on the M25, the sky was only just lightening. She drove in silence until she reached the M1 then taking the northbound exit, she switched on the car's radio. It was a golden oldie station and Paul McCartney & Wings were singing *My Love* and Poppy sang along.

She stopped at Watford services and checked her phone. She thought about ringing Uncle Michael but decided against it. She didn't want to tell him she was back. Not yet.

She got herself a McDonald's breakfast, complete with a very, very large coffee then got back on the road. The day was overcast and chilly. Typical English weather, she thought. She looked to the grey slate of the sky and smiled.

She kept the oldies station on and sang along to Bowie and Thin Lizzy and Queen. The music made Poppy think of her uncle and she wondered how he'd react to seeing her again. They spoke on the phone from time to time, but his hearing had gotten so bad in recent years that it'd become almost impossible; the conversation stilted and repetitive. Basically, she just spent the entire time shouting down the line at him. It would be comical if it weren't so frustrating.

Free's *All Right Now* came on and she turned the volume up. This wasn't her music of choice, but it felt good to be hearing these songs again. Fitting, she thought, to arrive back in England and hear the music of her childhood. The music that made her think of home.

Approaching Leicestershire, the sun broke through the cloud cover and Poppy saw the rolling fields of England in golden, autumnal light. It felt so strange to be back, after such a long time away. Strange, and yet, the sky, the fields, the cars, the feeling of the country, all felt so familiar.

The traffic got heavier as she approached Derbyshire and she ended up in a very slow moving jam before she reached junction 24. She was humming along to 10CC's *Rubber Bullets* when she entered Derby. The streets of her youth flashed by, all seemingly unchanged, and yet changed. The place looked smaller, more run-down. Shop fronts and pubs she used to know were now boarded up. The video shop was gone—because all video shops were now gone—the chippie was gone, the paper shop she knew.

She drove through Alvaston and took the by-pass up to Chaddesden. Once in Chad she pulled over in a side street and checked the map on her phone. She hoped that the address she'd been given was correct.

Poppy turned the radio off and continued on, following the directions on her phone; she was unfamiliar with this part of Chaddesden. She passed through the shops on the main street then took a right, then a left onto Hanbury Road. Her phone told her she had arrived at her destination and she parked up a few houses down from the one she wanted. She sat in the car and looked at the house—a run-down semi with peeling paint and a tatty door. The curtains were drawn and the place looked quiet.

She hoped she had the right house. And also hoped she had the wrong house.

She took a deep breath and got out of the car.

***

On Friday 27th August, 1976, a week after she moved into 2 Society Place, Heather Lowes began her job as a check-out girl at Presto's supermarket on Normanton Road. Her first shift was from 10a.m. to 3p.m. She arrived at 9:45a.m. and was given her uniform—a blue bib that she put over her own shirt and was given a name tag with HEATHER crudely written upon it. It was hot out, but thankfully the shop was cool, and also, relativity quiet.

The 'team leader' Carol—the woman who had interviewed Heather along with the manager Mr Sullivan—explained how to work the till with all the insight and patience of a toddler. "You press this one to open it," she said, pressing some button that Heather barely registered. The till opened and she immediately slammed it shut again. "All items are priced up and you have to key in every price individually. And make sure you put in the correct amount otherwise you have to void the entire thing and start again. I'll be keeping an eye on you. Right, sit down and show me what I've just shown you."

Heather sat down and tried to open the till, but pressed the wrong button. "No," said Carol. "This one," and stamped her finger down and the till flew out again. "Ten bobs go in there, fivers there, ones there, and all your change, your 2s, your 1s, your 5s go along here. Half-pees go there. Go it?"

"Yes," said Heather.

"Good. Right, open your till and get to work, I'll be back to check on you shortly."

Then Carol was gone. Heather removed the 'till closed' sign from her conveyor belt and waited for her first costumer. The woman on the till across from her smiled and said hello. Heather smiled back. The woman was plump, middle-aged, with a kindly face and jet black hair.

"Take no notice of old Carol. She's got a stick up her arse."

Heather laughed.

"Just ignore her," continued the woman. "She likes to throw her weight around, but she's just a glorified till girl herself. Sullivan only gave her the team leader role to shut her up about rotas. I'm Maggie, by the way."

"Heather."

"Pleased to meet you, Heather. We don't get many young uns like yourself working here. You local?"

"Yes, I've just moved into Society Place."

The woman—Maggie—frowned. "Society Place?"

"Yes."

"You not heard the stories about that street?"

**

Rafferty went out. He'd had enough of his bedroom, his mother, the TV: he'd had enough of hiding, so he went out on the street. Lee Cope was the only other kid out. He was fixing the chain on his bike, his hands greasy, sweat pouring off him. It was already scorching and wasn't even midday. Raff was dressed in a t-shirt and shorts, his arm slinged-up. There wasn't a cloud in the sky.

"Alright," he said, approaching Lee.

His friend looked up, squinting against the sun. "Ay up, Gilroy."

"What ya doin'?"

"Ah, chain keeps coming off." Lee turned to look at Raff, his eyes darting to the sling. "So...?"

Raff looked down at his arm. "This?"

"Well, yeah, course. Becky Philips reckoned you'd broken both your arms and your legs."

"She doesn't know what she's talking about."

"Yeah, she's a girl."

"Yeah."

"But...you did break that one?"

"Yeah."

"How did it feel?"

Rafferty frowned. "It hurt, Lee. The biggest hurt I've ever had."

"Wow," said Lee, suitably impressed.

"I cracked a rib and got loads of cuts and bruises as well."

"Let us see."

Rafferty held out both arms and turned them, pointing out various scabs and bruises. Then he turned and pointed out several down the back of his legs. Lee was very, very impressed.

"Got more on me back as well."

Lee's respect was absolute. "You must have really come down. How high were you?"

"High."

"Did you slip or summat?"

Raff didn't answer at first.

"Raff? What happened?"

"A branch. It...it snapped and I just fell."

"Wow. What was hospital like?"

"Boring. What's been happening out 'ere?"

"Nothin' much. Mal tried to cheat at footie and we gave him a pasting and Becky's been really annoying. We didn't think you'd be coming out again. We called for you loads."

"I know. I just didn't feel up to it."

Lee looked at the scabs on his arms and said, "Yeah, I bet it well killed."

"It did."

Lee stood up, his chain forgotten. "You wanna have a kick about?"

"I don't know. I got to be careful of me arm."

"Ah, go on. Just steady...me and you, before the others come out..."

"Alright, suppose."

Lee went inside to get his ball.

***

"What stories?"

"Oh, you know...silly stuff."

"No, I don't know. What stories?"

Maggie licked her lips then saw an old lady shuffle up to her lane. "I'll have to tell you later." Then she turned to speak to the old woman. "Mrs Crosby, how are you my love?"

Heather turned back to her till. A young mother was approaching her lane carrying a basket in one arm and a baby in the other. The mother looked tired and stressed. In fact, she looked like she hadn't slept for a week. She put her basket down on the end and began to place items on the conveyor with one hand, struggling to control the wriggling baby with the other.

Heather began pricing up the shopping. It took her some time to find the price tags on a few of the items, and then even longer to key in the correct amount in the till. The mother looked increasingly annoyed the longer Heather took, which flustered her even more. To add to the situation, the baby started crying.

Finally, the already frazzled mother said to Heather, "Look, can you hurry up please. My baby needs feeding."

Heather nodded her head and tried to rush. She keyed in the wrong amount on a tin of luncheon meat and didn't know what to do.

The mother said, "Oh, this is ridiculous."

The baby screamed and screamed and screamed.

Carol came and stood behind Heather. It wasn't even eleven o'clock.

***

They passed the ball back and forth, running to the curb each time they heard a car turn into Society Place. There was the drone of a plane overhead and Lee and Raff talked about football players and how annoying Becky Philips was and Lee wanted to know if Raff was allowed to stay up and watch *The Avengers*.

Lee kicked the ball hard and Raff ran to catch it, but it went past him, hit the curb, and bounced off down the street. Both boys ran after it.

The ball hit the boot of Mrs Newbold's Ford Anglia and shot back towards the boys. It was Lee who caught it. They inspected the car. No marks. They both laughed. That was when they heard the shouting.

They turned and both saw that the door to number 2 was wide open. From inside, Heather Lowes was shouting for help.

Rafferty understood that she sounded very frightened.

***

Maggie took Heather through the back. There were trolleys stacked with boxed goods, and shelves filled with products. Maggie also pointed out a large white door and said it was the walk-in freezer then she showed Heather into a grotty, window-less room with a garden table and a worktop with a kettle and some mould. There was an old gentleman sat at the table reading the paper. He had a shock of white hair and a craggy face.

"Harold, this is Heather. She's new."

Harold looked over his paper and smiled. "Ay up me duck. My, you're a spring chicken, ain't ya..."

"Hello," said Heather.

"That battleaxe out there bin givin' ya any jip?" said Harold.

Heather wasn't sure what to say. Thankfully, Maggie answered for her. "Ay, she's been on the warpath."

"I dunno, give em a bit of power and they go crazy with it," said Harold. "You take no notice of the old bag, love. I've seen them kind come and go, I tell ya."

"Okay," said Heather.

"Sit down," said Maggie. "Wanna brew?"

Heather sat down across from Harold. "Yes, please."

"Sugar?"

"Two please."

Maggie flicked on the kettle and rinsed two cups out in the sink. Harold returned to his paper. HOTTEST SUMMER ON RECORD read the headline; a girl in a tiny crochet bikini lay sprawled on a beach.

"Says ere Maggs, if you're gonna 'ave a bath you can only fill it with five inches of water."

Maggie looked over at Harold. "How the bleedin' hell you suppose to get clean in that trickle. Cuppa?"

"No," said Harold. "Just had one. They're also saying you should pour your washing up water down the toilet instead of flushing it."

"Give over. That's ridiculous."

"Well if the weather carries on like this, Maggs, it's only gonna get worse. It hasn't rained for two months. Not anywhere in England. Two months, Maggs. Says it 'ere. What can't speak, can't lie."

"I never thought I'd see the day when I'd actually want it to rain. My lawn's gone brown. And these ladybirds are a bleeding nuisance."

"They're a plague Margaret, plain and simple."

Maggie poured the tea then sat down next to Heather. "It's just mashin'," she said.

"Thanks."

Heather wanted to ask Maggie what she'd heard about Society Place but with Harold there she felt shy and in no way comfortable in broaching the subject.

"So..." Maggie began. "You married, Heather?"

***

Rafferty froze at the door. Heather Lowes was still calling from somewhere in the house. She sounded very distressed. Lee was at his side, peering into the front room, his eyes wide, his head darting about. The cellar door was open.

"She's down in the cellar," said Lee. "We better go and help her."

Lee shoved him, but Raff remained clinging to the doorframe.

"Come on," said Lee.

"We should go and get help," said Raff.

Help! Please help me!

"She sounds like she's in a lot of trouble, Raff. We should go down there."

Help!

She sounded more than in trouble. She sounded scared. Very scared, and Rafferty really didn't want to know why.

Lee shoved past him and stepped into the front room. He stopped by the chair and looked back at Rafferty. "You coming or what?"

Help me please!

Raff looked down at his finger poking out of the plaster cast. They were twitching. Sweat ran down his forehead and he wiped it with his good hand.

Please God! Somebody help me!

Raff stepped into the house.

***

Carol burst into the staffroom and scolded both Heather and Maggie (but mainly Heather) for being sat on their backsides when there were customers queuing at the tills.

Heather was glad of the intrusion.

"Well, Lyn and Grainne are out there..." said Maggie. "And beside, we've still got five minutes of our break left."

"Not by my watch, now come on!"

Carol left, slamming the door behind her.

"Come on," said Maggie. "We better go or we'll never hear the end of it."

On the way out, old Harold said, "That woman needs taking down a peg or two."

Heather went back to her till and started work, picking up speed as she went along.

She had three and a half hours left of her shift.

***

"HELP ME!" screamed Heather Lowes.

The two boys stood at the top of the cellar stairs. The woman was down there and it was dark. Rafferty didn't like the *feeling* that emanated from down in that solid dark; his every sense telling him that something was very wrong. After the brightness of the day outside, it truly looked like a solid wall of darkness. It swallowed the bottom steps. It was all consuming.

They heard Heather whimpering, then, very softly, *"Rafferty? Is that you?"*

Lee shot him a look, but Raff's eyes remained fixed on the darkness.

"Rafferty, please help me...I've tripped and fallen. Please help..."

He glanced back to the front door, still open, and to the sunshine world out there. A world of kick-abouts on the street, ice cream vans, scrumping, bike rides, comics, TV, mum and dad, school, Becky Philips, *Doctor Who* on Saturday nights. A world of the familiar, the real, the ordinary. Down in the cellar, however, in the dark, there was something else. Something far from ordinary. Something that, once seen, may never be unseen. This much Rafferty understood. To go down in that cellar, was to leave the world he knew behind, forever.

"Please help me, Rafferty..."

He lowered his foot onto the top step. Lee didn't move.

Rafferty took one last look at the sunshine world then descended into the cellar.

Into the darkness.

***

Poppy Lowes scanned the street up and down. There was no one about. Leaves scattered along the pavement. The sky, low and grey. Autumn in England, she thought. It'd been a long time. There was a nip in the air and she buttoned up her coat. She looked to the house. It lay in stillness.

She walked around the front of the car to the pavement. Far up the street she saw a woman wheeling out her bin to the end of her front wall. Her boundary. The woman was the first sign of life Poppy had seen on Hanbury Road.

She approached the house. The curtains in the top windows were also drawn. This was a house that wanted to keep the world out. A fortress, a sanctuary, a protective cocoon made from bricks and mortar.

She reached the house and stood before it. The wind kicked up, leaves cackled along the pavement. Poppy stood a step over the boundary and composed herself. She knocked on the door three times before she heard chains being unlatched, and locks being turned.

The door opened, only slightly, and a face appeared. A gaunt, haunted face, with dark eyes and deep lines and thinning hair, and a prominent cleft lip. The eyes looked slightly vacant, if not a little sad.

She knew the man was only nine years older than herself but he looked a good twenty years older.

She gave a thin smile and said, "Rafferty Gilroy? I'm Poppy Lowes."

CHAPTER SIXTEEN

Chloe Gilroy wanted a drink. Just one. Just to see her through the rest of the afternoon. She checked the drinks cupboard, knowing full well she'd already polished off the vodka, then she checked upstairs, under the bed, but that bottle was also empty. "Fuck," she said, running her hands through her hair. She caught sight of her reflection in the mirror above her dresser. She didn't like what she saw.

Chloe approached herself, pulling at the skin beneath her eyes, checking the crow's feet, the bags, the tiredness, the emptiness. She used to think herself attractive, and she certainly got plenty of attention when she was younger, but now, she felt ugly. Ugly and old. Having a child had fucked up her body. Her stomach used to be hard, flat, tight, now it was doughy and lined with stretch marks. She tried to keep active and eat right—although difficult living with a man that just wanted to eat pie and chips every night—and when Rafferty was younger she used to take him to the Arboretum and run around with him, but her stomach never tightened. It was just the way her body was now. Rich had made the odd comment every now and again, but he didn't seem to mind it when he came up to bed after the snooker.

Raising Rafferty had aged her. She was not yet twenty-nine but felt she looked at least thirty-nine. There were the lines around her eyes of course, and the ever-increasing greys she kept finding in her black hair—these she'd pull out immediately—and most upsetting of all, the dark, puffy bags under her eyes. Her skin looked dry, her breasts were no longer firm, and her pelvic floor was still fucked after pushing a ten pound baby out nine years before. Rafferty had been a monster. In her darker moments she found herself hating the boy, actively despising him for what he'd done to her. But it was a fleeting hatred, for she loved the boy. He was a hand-full, but then, every mother she knew with a son said the same. She loved his cleft lip, and his hair, and the back of his neck, his shoulder blades, his nature, his joy in such an otherwise joyless house.

She turned her back on her reflection and went out the door, across the top of the stairs and into Rafferty's room. The window was open, the breeze gently moving the curtains. Raff's bed was unmade and she shook her head. She'd told him time and time again to make his bed before he went anywhere, but he hardly ever did. She knew he didn't do this purposely; he just got distracted thinking about the day ahead. He got excited about things.

Chloe smiled and went over to the bed. She pulled the cover back and then saw the stain. She wrinkled her nose, then bent and lightly touched the dark patch. Wet. She bent further and smelt the bed and this confirmed it. She straightened up, wondering why he hadn't told her he'd wet the bed; he normally did, but now she thought about it, he had been quiet at breakfast and hadn't eaten much of his Sugar Puffs. She'd been surprised when he said he was going out the front to play. He'd not left the house since his accident and he was beginning to get right under her feet. She thought he'd never go back out again before school started back up. Chloe didn't push him too much though, for she knew, deep down, that he was frightened of the house at the end of the road. She knew this because she was also frightened of it. Always had been.

She began to strip the bed when there came a sudden knocking on the front door. As all the windows in the house where open she could hear a boy's voice shouting, "Mrs Gilroy...Mrs Gilroy...please come...it's Raff!"

Oh God, she thought, what now?

She raced downstairs, the boy continually banging on the door.

"Mrs Gilroy...come quickly..."

Chloe flew open the front door and there was little Lee Cope looking pale and frightened.

"Please...Mrs Gilroy..."

"Where is he?" she said, but somehow she already knew the answer.

***

Heather left Presto's at three fifteen. The afternoon had gone better than the morning. She got the hang of the till and developed a kind of rhythm in pricing up items. Before long she was chatting with customers (most regulars inquiring as to who she was) and gassing with Maggie across the way. She found she even enjoyed herself. It was nice to be out, doing something, meeting people, feeling like herself again. Carol came around once or twice trying to pick faults, and although she made the odd comment, there wasn't really much she could say. What she did say was trivial, minor, hardly worth mentioning and Heather just smiled brightly and said thank you for the advice. This response never failed to completely throw bullies like Carol. They never knew what to make of it—a smile and a thank you, that is. Bullies like to make people feel small, they like to find a weak spot and prod and prod and prod until your defences are completely shot. Heather was taught to always respond with a big smile, sprinkled with some overbearing gratitude, and it confuses the hell out of them. It worked every time. Sure enough, after several beaming smiles and bordering-on-sarcastic thank yous, Carol no longer came around to Heather's till. Maggie watched this play in awe.

"I love it! You've utterly bamboozled her," she said.

"Kill them with kindness," said Heather. "That's what my mother always used to say."

"It's genius."

She felt good after having done a day's work. The sun was bright and hot, kids were out on the streets, car radios blasted out, the music box jingle of an ice cream van could be heard in the distance—*half a pound of tuppenny rice, half a pound of treacle*—and women stood out on pavements and talked in huddles.

Heather walked through this summer scene, her mind drifting. She thought of the summers of her girlhood, of playing hide and seek with her brother in the garden, and her father in his shed, tinkering with his motorbike, the radio on, the Beatles singing *From Me To You*, her mother bringing out lemonade for them all. She knew it wasn't always that idyllic, but nostalgia has a way of shaping the past into packaged bliss. A memory formed of feeling rather than truth. Also, the fact that her parents were no longer alive made these memories all the more poignant and bittersweet, and it is that sense of times gone, lost forever, that gives nostalgia its halcyon glow. It bathes the past in golden light, edging out the darkness, and the fears, and the trauma of childhood.

She turned onto Society Place from the opposite end to where her house stood. Any good feeling she had that afternoon evaporated immediately. She lived in a haunted house, and no matter how bright the sun, how joyous the sounds of summer were, the fact remained she now lived in a constant state of fear. It rose in her like a black wave.

She continued walking, trying to roll the wave back, turning over in her mind the question of what could be done about the thing in her house. The idea of getting a priest in crossed her mind, but she thought it too outlandish, something that only happened in the movies, but then doubled back and she thought, why not? Why not get the house blessed? She wasn't a religious person, not in any orthodox sense anyway. She hadn't been to church since childhood, but wasn't an atheist either. Gnosticism was perhaps more where her feelings lay—the thought that there was something beyond this world, but what, she couldn't say.

Another thought lodged in her brain then. From something Mrs Green said. If her house was truly haunted, then, in a strange kind of way, it could be seen as a hopeful phenomenon, for any experience of the paranormal is a glimpse into life beyond death, surely? For Heather, there was a comfort in that idea. As an orphan and a widow, life after death was truly something to hope for.

Except...

This hope was short-lived. The black wave rose up once more when Heather saw Rafferty Gilroy's mother step out from her house carrying the limp body of a child in her arms.

***

"What did you see down in that cellar?"

Rafferty Gilroy leaned back in his chair. Poppy sat across from him, her hands in her lap. They were sat at a dining table in the back room, the curtain open a little at the middle, allowing a shaft of light to lance in. It divided them.

"You come all the way from California to ask me that?" he said.

Poppy looked through the gap in the curtains, to the overgrown garden beyond. "It's one of the reasons, yes."

"You seen your uncle?"

"Not yet."

Rafferty nodded. He looked gaunt, straggly, unwell. Heather noted that the last time she saw him, about two decades before, he hadn't looked like this. She guessed him to be about fifty-two, fifty-three now, but he looked sixty, at least. His nose had grown bulbous, altering his features entirely. There was a redness that spread from his nose to his cheek bones. His hair was long and dirty; he looked (and smelt) like he hadn't washed in a good while. His teeth were yellow, his skin ashen. It struck Poppy that he looked like he was dying.

"Why can't you just let it go?" he said to her.

She looked at him, hard. "You know why."

He didn't say anything. The light shifted—clouds passing over the face of the sun—and across from her, Rafferty darkened. The light made Poppy think of an old gangster film. A film noir. Rafferty Gilroy began to talk.

***

Heather ran to her house (holding her stomach all the way). Mrs Gilroy dropped to her knees, her boy still in her arms. There was another boy behind Mrs Gilroy—a boy Heather had seen playing out on the street. He looked stricken.

Mrs Gilroy was gently rocking her son when Heather reached them.

"Oh my God, is he okay?"

Mrs Gilroy looked at Heather, her expression blank. Rafferty was still, his eyes closed. He was breathing, Heather was relieved to see. Unconscious then?

"What happened?" said Heather, but Rafferty's mother still didn't say anything.

"It was the shape…" said the boy behind Mrs Gilroy. His eyes were wide, full of terror. "…it pulled him into the hole…"

"Hole? Where?"

"In your cellar, Miss…"

Rafferty coughed and lurched upwards, his mother almost losing her grip on him. He opened his eyes, but he didn't appear to be seeing the world around him. He was still seeing something internal. Raff screamed and his mother held him and kept repeating "It's okay, it's okay, Mummy's here…it's all over…" but still the boy screamed.

Instinctively Heather reached out and placed her hand on Rafferty's good arm. The connection startled the boy and he turned and stared straight at her.

The intensity of his look caused Heather to let go of his arm and stumble back onto her behind. Rafferty remained fixed on her.

He said, "The man in your house is bad. He wants to play not very nice games."

CHAPTER SEVENTEEN

"I feel old now," said Rafferty, looking to the gap in the curtains, to the spill of light. "Older than my years...I know I look it." Poppy passed no comment. "I've lived alone for a long time and I know I've become set in my ways. I realise how I look to you...the way I live..."

"What happened down in my mother's cellar, Rafferty?"

"Why do you want to know so badly? It happened over forty years ago. Some ghosts need to be put to rest."

Poppy looked at him. "Not this one, Rafferty. This one won't rest. And you know that..."

Rafferty looked at his hands. There was dirt under his long nails.

"Me and a friend of mine, Lee Cope, were out kicking a ball about. I'd broken my arm from falling out of a tree and was feeling pretty sorry for myself that summer. And it was quite a summer...so hot..." He looked at her. "Your mother's front door was open and we could hear her shouting for help from somewhere in the house. Lee went in first and...your mother's cries for help were coming from down in the cellar. The cellar door was open and I guess Lee and I went down there, although I have no recollection of doing that. My memory sharpens at the image of me and Lee being stood in that cellar, looking at a dark tunnel that ran under the house. Like a chamber. There were bricks all around the hole, as if something had kicked it open."

He swallowed hard, his eyes glistening.

"What was in the hole, Rafferty?"

He looked her. A rabbit in the headlights. "I was," he said.

"You?"

"Me as I am now, only I didn't know it was me at the time. But every time I see myself in a mirror, I see the face I saw in that tunnel."

"I don't understand."

"Nor do I, but that is what I saw. We both peered into the hole, drawn to it for reasons beyond natural comprehension. We were *pulled* to it. Lee stumbled on the bricks and fell back and that is when the hand reached out and grabbed me. It snatched me into the tunnel. Into the dark. I could hear Lee screaming for me, but I couldn't see him. I could only see the milky white arm that gripped me, dragging me deeper and deeper into the tunnel. I heard Lee running back up the cellar stairs and across the house and out of the front door, but it was a faraway sound. I was conscious of him leaving me, but also unconscious of it. For that long moment of terror, I felt I existed in two realms. Have you ever had sleep paralysis, Poppy?"

"Yes."

"Then you know...that sense of awareness of the physical world around you, but being completely locked into the dark. Not being able to move a muscle. Screaming in your head for help and no one able to hear you. It's a deathly feeling. That was how I felt in that tunnel. I was locked into the dark. Unable to move...the terror was all consuming...a paralysis of fear. The face came into view...my face. That craggy old beaten to shit face I have now. It came close, breathed its rancid dead air into me.

"I saw my future. My entire miserable life mapped out. Can you imagine that? Being nine years old and the sense of wonder and optimism you have at that age being sucked from you in an instant..."

"I can, yes."

Rafferty nodded. She understood him.

"If there is such a thing as a soul, then the thing in the hole sucked mine away, leaving the empty husk you see before you. I saw the person I am today, a half person, shut away from the world. Someone waiting for death, but also fearing it beyond all thought and reason. I didn't truly understand at the time, but the thing in the hole...that thing with my future face...showed me who I would become. It also showed me how I am to die. Here, in this chair. Alone."

He looked at Poppy.

"It showed me what is waiting for me...at the threshold."

"What was that thing in the cellar?"

"It was something very old...ancient, in fact. Something that never lived...was never human. An entity beyond our understanding. It understands us though. It plays with us, toys with us like a cat batting around a mouse. To the outside it looks playful, but claws and teeth are slowly killing the mouse. With me, it took away any chance I had of a good life...a happy life. It drained away my humanity down in that tunnel. I came out broken…a hollow human. And I've lived empty ever since. When I was younger I drowned myself in drugs, sex, booze…I did everything I could to try and feel something, but hollow I remained. Now, the only thing I do feel is fear. That is something I really can feel, for I know what waits for me."

He looked to the dust caught in the light spill.

"It also showed me something else?" he said.

"I'm listening…"

"It showed me your mother, and it showed me the baby growing inside your mother. You, Poppy. It showed me that it wanted you."

***

Mrs Gilroy took her boy inside. Lee Cope went running home. Heather sat on her front step, not wanting to go inside the house. Cars went by, a plane droned overhead. She heard a police siren far off. The hum of life all around her, but in the house behind her—silence. Unnaturally deadened.

Mrs Gilroy came out of her house and walked back down the street towards Heather.

Heather stood up to greet her. "Is he alright?" she asked.

"I've put him to bed. He's sleeping. There are some marks on his arm, but otherwise he's fine. Physically anyway."

"I can't understand it. I don't know how…"

"Come off it, Mrs Lowes. We both know there is something wrong with your house."

Heather looked at her, stunned.

"You should come to see me," said Mrs Gilroy. "My name is Chloe. I have to fix dinner now. My husband will be home soon, but no doubt he'll be out to the pub after so you come over later...at eight."

"Okay...I will."

"And Mrs Lowes..."

"Please, call me Heather."

"Heather. If that thing in there touches my boy again, I will burn your house down."

CHAPTER EIGHTEEN

Rafferty watched Poppy Lowes drive away, then he pulled the curtain back across the window, blocking out the world again. He went and sat in his chair for a long time then he went upstairs to his bedroom.

The curtains here were drawn also. The light glowing around the edges of the material. Dust lay over surfaces, mould in high corners. There were no pictures, no mirrors, no books or trinkets, any ornaments of any kind. There was a bed, looking in dire need of a change, and a rail with a few clothes hung. That was it.

Beneath the bed, however, was a suitcase, and it was this that Rafferty pulled free. He placed it on the bed and opened it up.

Inside were items from the childhood that he had shut away. There was his birth certificate and a commemorative plate marking his entrance into the world. It showed a stork carrying a baby to its crib and had Rafferty's name, time and date of birth inscribed around its edges. There was an out of date passport, never used, and other forms of documentation. These were not what Rafferty was looking for however. He ruffled through and then found an envelope. This he picked out then sat on the bed, envelope in hand. It was a long while before he opened it.

When he finally did open it, he pulled free a half dozen or so photographs. The first was of his mother, Chloe, stood by a railing on a sunny day. It was taken when she was pregnant with Raff in the summer of 1967. She was young and beautiful. The photograph was worn, they all were, all tinged with that faded glow, like they were capturing a half-remembered dream, rather than snapshots in time. The next was a picture of his mother and father, years later, and the spark was gone from his mother's eyes. She was still beautiful but she didn't seem present. The lights had been turned off. His father on the other hand was smiling but there was no warmth in it.

The next picture was of Rafferty, taken in the summer of 1975 when he was eight years old. The summer before it happened. He stared at the boy he used to know, and wondered what happened to him.

Rafferty hadn't even told Poppy Lowes about the Once-Man who dragged him down to the hole for a second time, to the nest of ghosts. He didn't tell her that when he finally escaped he didn't speak for five years, driving his mother to complete despair and ruin. He told her about his excesses in his twenties, but not in any great detail. He didn't tell her that the late 1980s were a haze of substance abuse, alcoholism, bouts of homelessness, petty crimes, insatiable sex with both women and men, and violent rages, all done in an effort to feel something. But no feeling ever came even after his mother died in 1991 of cancer. His father had died before that, but he didn't give a fuck about his father. Nor did his mother, who divorced him in 1981.

He didn't tell her that he knew what they had to do but he figured she'd be back before long. Once she figured it out for herself.

He looked at the boy, the cleft lip clearly noticeable; his eyes wide and bright and full of life. The boy was in a park, a ball in his hand, smiling, baring all teeth. He looked at the photograph for a long time.

He wondered who that boy might have become had he lived.

CHAPTER NINETEEN

The singer was late as usual. The rest of Candlestick Park set up their gear, tuned up then all fell into a jam. Michael lead the way with a bluesy riff he'd been playing around with. Paul Raisey quickly found a bass line and Bill picked up the beat. Once the rhythm section was locked in, Michael began soloing. The band had been together so long that playing off one another was second nature. They were tight and could lock into a groove at the drop of a hat. Pete was always late—a singer's prerogative, he once told Michael—and the band would warm up by jamming before he arrived. Very often, it was Michael's favourite time. He could try out riffs and simply fly without always being second guessed by his singer. And Paul and Bill were a great rhythm unit, allowing Michael to experiment with sounds and ideas.

The band rehearsed in an abandoned factory on the outskirts of Darley Park. They shared the space with several other local bands—all locked into their rehearsal time by a rota overseen by the building's owner, a gruff barrel of a man called Dave. The space was on the second floor. There were no windows, but there was strip lighting and egg boxes for sound proofing all over the walls. Candlestick Park usually had a gig Friday nights but not that week. Nor were they playing Saturday night. In fact, they weren't booked to play anywhere for the next two weekends, so they'd decided to use this gap in their schedule to work on some new songs. Some original new songs.

Michael had been pushing for them to try more and more original material for a long while. He had amassed quite a songbook since joining the band two years before, and although he'd managed to slip a few of his songs in—most notably *Hey Girl*—they'd been reluctant to sway from their steady diet of rock and pop covers in case the bookings dried up. But Michael had his sights set on taking the band a lot further than the Red Lion in Heanor. He wanted the band to start rehearsing originals, road testing them in front of audiences, and then once tight, laying down some demos to send out to record companies.

Bill was initially the most vocal in deriding this plan. "They come and see us to hear Bowie and the Sabbs not some stuff they don't know the words to," he'd said, but after they'd road-tested *Hey Girl* and it went down a storm he started to change his mind. And Michael had been priming them all summer, showing them new riffs, lyric ideas and eventually entire songs. One new song, *You Never Know*, was a riff Michael brought in, which they jammed and which Pete made up lyrics to on the spot. *You never know what the day will bring*, he snarled. It was a rocker; just over two minutes, fast, blistering, beautiful in its aggression. They'd tried it out at Talk of the Midlands and it went down like gang busters. That was the real turning point. So with this gap in their gigs, they'd all made a collective decision to work on more new material. And if the singer ever turned up, they could get started.

The jam came to an abrupt halt when Michael broke a string. "Fuck," he said.

"You were thrashing her too hard, Mike," said Bill from behind his kit.

Michael played a Gibson SG and she could take some hammer but strings were regular casualties once he started soloing. He didn't use a pick and had a way of playing that pulled and jabbed at the strings, which meant he always he had to carry spare strings on him. He put his guitar down and opened his case, looking for the right replacement string—a D.

Bill came out from behind the kit and Paul twiddled around on his bass.

"Paul told us you had him cleaning out your sister's cellar," said Bill.

Michael stopped what he was doing and looked at him, then glanced at Paul. He was still running through a bass line and didn't notice them talking.

"Did he," said Michael. "What else did he tell you?"

"Nothing," said Bill but he looked sheepish and Michael didn't believe him.

Paul checked his tuning again then slipped the strap over his head and put the bass down, carefully leaning it against his amp. He walked over to the others. "Where is he?"

"Dunno," Bill said. "He gets worse. I was hoping we could get down for last orders."

"What did you think to that riff we were just playing around with?" said Michael.

"Yeah, alright," said Paul. "A bit Led Zepp like."

"Yeah," agreed Bill, not really caring one way or the other. "That a new tune?"

"Could be."

Although his rhythm section was tight, Michael knew that when it came to original material they needed a lot more guidance. They could be inventive within the confines of a song, but lacked vision when it came to shaping a new piece of music. Basically, they weren't writers; they couldn't come up with tunes themselves, and sometimes, even when presented with a new chord structure or musical framework, they struggled to see its potential. Whereas Pete was very good at taking an idea and twisting it, shaping it into a fully formed song. It was a craft. A craft Michael and Peter understood instinctively but that Paul and Bill could never quite grasp. Often Michael would tell Paul what to play. However, with Bill it was a little different. He could get quite barbed if told what to play. Michael and Peter had felt his wrath on more than one occasion at so much as suggesting a change to his playing, so they didn't do it anymore. He was a solid drummer though, so it wasn't too much of an issue, except in his general lack of vision for what Candlestick Park could become.

Pete was a different matter. He was born to be a rock star. Cocksure, good-looking, charming, and laced with an air of danger that made him extremely attractive to the opposite sex. His was a clear vision and he was living it every day. He didn't work, not in the conventional sense anyway but could be seen out and about, wheeling and dealing, selling this and that to get by. He signed-on as well and somehow charmed the girls down at the dole office into keeping his money coming in, no questions asked. Michael had known him since school and he'd always been the same, even when he was a little kid. He was always the leader, always the one with the plan. Before she'd died, Michael's mother had remarked that Pete Stringer would either make it to the very top, or kill himself trying, and Michael knew there was a bitter truth it that. It was all or nothing for Pete, and Michael was prepared to go all the way with him even if it meant they crashed and burned.

Pete had asked Michael to join Candlestick Park when their first guitarist hadn't cut the mustard. "He couldn't play the solo to *Moonage Daydream* so we gave him the boot," he'd told Michael, and so Michael joined. He'd been in bands before but Candlestick Park was a proper working band. They were out every weekend and week nights too. Michael and Pete had lost touch a little after school but once they started playing together they immediately clicked. They understood one another, and they understood the music. It was inevitable that they would start writing.

And so, always one to make an entrance, Pete Stringer burst into the rehearsal room half an hour late, arms aloft, proclaiming, "I've done it, lads! I've cracked it!"

Bill looked over his cymbals and said, "What's he bleedin' on about?"

"Lord knows," said Michael.

Pete came bounding over. "Check this out, I've booked us some studio time."

There was a collective, "What?"

"So I know this bloke called Tim, who knows this guy Phil Ward, who owns a studio out near Ashbourne. He told me that this Phil Ward had seen us when we played Cleo's the other week, when we supported The Groundhogs, remember? Anyway, apparently he really thought we had something with *Hey Girl*. Tim told me he couldn't get it outta his head all week. Right catchy he said. Any road, I calls him up like, this afternoon, told him who I were, and he remembered us right off the bat. He started singing *Hey Girl* down the phone to me."

"Fuck off?" said Bill.

"God's honest. He said he'd give us the studio for free to lay it down on the proviso that he gets to produce it."

Michael sat down on his amp. "You serious?"

"Deadly, mate. He said he'd keep next weekend open for us. This could be it, man. He might even give us enough time to get a couple of tracks down. *You Never Know* maybe? Or *Our Green God*."

Paul piped up. "I think I've got something on next weekend with the missus."

"Oh, give over," said Pete. "What could be more important than this?"

"Well...I think it's her mum's birthday..."

Pete deflated. "And? Fuckin' hell, Paul, this is our birthday. Chances like this don't come around every day, y'know."

"I know…it's just…I'll have to clear it with her."

Pete rubbed his forehead then turned to Michael. "What you think?"

Michael looked up at him. "I think it's…I think it's great, man. Fuckin' great. Let's 'ave it."

Pete beamed. "Yes, come on!" he said, bumping his fists. Then he turned to the drummer.

"Bill?"

"Yeah…sounds grand," was all he offered on the subject.

"Right then," said Pete, rubbing his hands together. "We better rattle through these tunes then. Get 'em as tight as a sixteen year's old cunny."

Michael winced.

They played *Hey Girl* twice on the bounce. During the song, Michael allowed himself to think of where all this might take him.

He dared to dream.

CHAPTER TWENTY

"Do you want a drink?" asked Chloe Gilroy.

"I'll have a water, please," said Heather.

"Water? Oh yeah, I forgot you're in the family way."

They were stood in Chloe's kitchen. The back door was open, dusk was coming on. Chloe got two glasses out from a cupboard: filled one up with water from the tap—which she handed to Heather—then fixed a gin and tonic in the other. The house was quiet. It smelt of joss sticks and cigarettes. Chloe had the kitchen light on, making the room sharp against the darkening world outside.

Her G&T fixed, she led Heather back through to the front room. There was patterned throws over the sofa and a sheepskin rug before the fireplace. The front curtains were drawn and a lamp with a red blub cast the room in low light. Heather sat on the sofa across from Chloe, who took the chair. Heather looked to the joss stick burning. There was also a full ashtray. Heather noted that the place wasn't untidy exactly but was in desperate need of a good clean. Chloe gulped much of her G&T down in one then sparked up a cigarette.

"My husband goes out most nights to the pub. I don't mind really; I like the peace and quiet."

"Right."

"So how did you husband die?"

Heather was a little startled by the woman's directness. "He died in a car crash. Head-on collision. Two other people died. It was their fault."

"That's a shit deal. I'm sorry."

"Yeah…" said Heather, looking to the floor. "It was a shit deal."

"Did he know?"

Heather looked at her and Chloe motioned to her belly.

"No." She touched her bump. "No, he didn't know. I didn't know until after he was dead."

"Jesus…I can't imagine…"

"You know what's strange?"

"What's that?"

"He only died five months ago and recently…recently it's sometimes difficult to picture him. Like have a real clear image of him in my mind. I have to really think hard."

Chloe watched her, taking a long drag on her cigarette.

"I hope my girl looks like him. So I can see him through her."

"How do you know it's going to be a girl?"

"I don't know…I just do."

"I can understand that. I knew Raff was going to be a boy."

"You must have had him young?"

"I was eighteen. Rich was twenty-four."

"That is young."

"It is, yes…" Chloe stumped her nub-end into the overflowing ashtray by her chair.

Heather drank a little of her water and placed it on a coaster on top of the gas fire.

She felt the baby kick and smiled a little. "How is Rafferty?" she asked.

Chloe didn't say anything at first, just stared at Heather, which quite unnerved her. Then she spoke, her voice low. "He slept most of the afternoon then I got him up for his tea but he hardly touched it. I gave him a bath then read him a story. I don't normally read to him anymore but tonight...tonight he seemed so much like a little boy again. He was very quiet. Hardly said anything. I stayed with him until he fell asleep again."

"I'm so sorry."

"It wasn't your fault..."

"I know, but...it happened in my house, so I feel responsible."

"There's only one person responsible, and it isn't you Heather."

"Shaw?"

Chloe's eyes widened. "Yes. How do you..."

"Mrs Green."

"I see. How much do you know?"

"Hardly anything. I knew he was a young man who lived in my house in the early sixties and he..."

"He what?"

"He was interested in the occult..."

"That's one way of putting it," said Chloe. She lit up another cigarette. "He was before my time but I've heard all the stories. Did Mrs Green tell you about the cats?"

"The cats? No."

"Well, after he moved in all the cats around here started disappearing. Mr Newbold's cat went, I know that, and a few others on the street. And cats from Silver Hill Lane and Corporation Street. Turns out he was catching them. He'd lure them into his house. He'd put treats out and they'd wander in like cats do and he trapped and killed them. Skinned them. Can you believe that?"

"That's so horrible."

"Apparently after he left, they found furs and bones in the house."

Heather sat forward, breathing deeply.

"You okay?" asked Chloe.

"Just…feel a bit sick."

"Oh, okay…do you want…"

Heather took a large drink of water, draining the glass.

"Do you want any more?"

"No…I'm fine now, thank you." She sat back and breathed out. "It just shocked me that's all. Thinking about how something like that happened in my…in my home."

"I know, I'm sorry, I didn't think, sometimes I just blurt stuff out."

"It's okay. You know, we found animal bones down in my cellar…"

"Really?"

"Yes. And there were strange markings and writings on all the walls down there."

Chloe sat back, taking this in then she said. "We moved here in 1968, after we got married…just before Raff was born. He was gone by then and the house was empty. There was a tramp in there for a while…"

"A tramp?"

"Yeah, but he didn't stay long. Someone did buy it in about 1969...could have been in the spring of '70...they bought it to do up. Wallpapered, gave it a lick of paint, but they couldn't sell it. I think it got repossessed in the end, so it fell into a kind of limbo. I never thought anyone would live there...until you showed up."

"You know the funny thing?" said Heather.

"What?"

"When we first came to look around it, Tony said the place felt...it felt good."

Chloe thought on this then said, "I think it wanted you to feel that. I mean...do you feel that still?"

"No," said Heather. "No, I don't."

Chloe sat forward in her chair, pulling on her cigarette. She blew out from the side of her mouth, then said, "What have you seen, Heather?"

Heather didn't answer at first. She ran a hand across her belly, then said, "It's not what I've seen, because I haven't really seen anything...it's what I've felt."

"What have you felt?"

"I've felt..." Heather became aware of the tears falling down her face. "I've felt something evil in my house. Something very bad...and I don't know what to do."

Chloe watched her sob. She didn't move, didn't speak, just stared.

Heather wiped her eyes, apologised then thought it absurd how the English always apologise for exhibiting emotions. She composed herself and met Chloe Gilroy's eyes. "Why didn't anyone tell me? Why do you all talk in riddles?" She felt anger rising and it felt good. Chloe remained silent, so Heather continued. "Everyone seems to know about my house, but me. Why is that, ah? Why is that every time I tell someone where I live they give me this look—a look of pity, a look of...fear. I started a new job today. At Presto's, on the check out. And there's this woman who works there and you should have seen her face when I told her I live on Society Place. You know what she said to me?" Heather didn't wait for an answer. "She said, *haven't you heard the stories about that street*? Just like that. Then went quiet on the subject, I mean...what the fuck is that, eh? You all know something and for some reason you're not telling me. Now why? What are you all hiding?"

"It's not that we're hiding anything, it's just..."

"Just what?"

"Just...everyone 'round here thought it was over..."

"Thought what was over? Just tell me straight, for God's sake."

"Alright. You wanna know?"

"Yes."

"Fine. It isn't just your house that's haunted. It's the whole fucking street. You got that? It has always been here. Shaw certainly didn't help matters but he was just some damn kid dabbling in the dark arts, thinking he was fucking Aleister Crowley or somethin'. Whatever haunts your house was there before

Shaw moved in. Shaw just opened the door a little wider, that's all. He opened the box and all sorts of things came tumbling out and they spread down Society Place. Some are benevolent—the little girl I've seen in Rafferty's room has never done us any harm. Mr Newbold's ghost is a little more problematic. That one moves things. Rearranges furniture, hides his keys, smashes the odd glass. I've been there when both his kitchen chairs shot across the tiles. Old Newbold talks to it. He calls it Simon. He's a lonely old man."

"So you're saying I live, not just in a haunted house but a haunted street."

"Yes."

"That's ridiculous."

"Is it? Why?"

"Well…it's…look…it's   hard   enough believing in one ghost, let alone a street full of them."

"If there can be one ghost, surely there can be more?"

Heather looked at her. "But why the secrecy?"

"Look…there has been a lot of talk about this street over the years, but the folk who live here,   in   these   houses,   we   keep our…experiences to ourselves. It's one thing to have locals gossiping, it'd be another thing having journalists knocking at the door looking for the latest sensation. We had one fella sniffing around a few years back when *The Exorcist* came out. My husband seen him on his way. He didn't come back." Chloe sat forward. "The thing is Heather, you've just moved in. We couldn't very well have you show up and immediately say, *Hello, welcome to the street, by the way, your house is haunted…all our houses are haunted, but yours is the worst.* You'd think us crazy?"

"Is it?" asked Heather.

"Is it what?"

"The worst?"

"If your question is whether the thing in your house is the worst entity on the street, then, yes…yes, it is."

Heather felt tears brimming again, but she bit them back. They both fell silent. There was a thud on the ceiling above them. They both looked up, then at each other.

"Rafferty?" asked Heather.

Chloe shook her head. "No…that's our room. It happens all the time. You get used to it."

Suddenly there was another noise. A key entered a lock, the front door opening inwards. Heather noticed Chloe squeeze her eyes shut for a brief moment.

In walked a large man. He looked a lot older than Chloe. He was stocky and had long hair, although it was receding on top. He filled the room with his bulk and from the way he swayed Heather surmised that he was quite inebriated.

He tried to focus on his wife and then carefully moved his head across to Heather. Chloe stood. "Richard, this is Heather from number 2. She was just leaving."

Heather stood up, "Yes, yes, I was just going."

Richard didn't seem to register any of this. Finally, he said, "I think I fancy a fry-up."

"Yes," said Chloe. "I'll rustle something up."

"Ay, and don't go scrimping on the bacon this time."

With that he stumbled off into the kitchen and Chloe rushed Heather to the door.

At the step, Chloe said, "Take back control of your house, Heather. Make it yours."

Then before Heather could say anything, Chloe Gilroy closed the door on her.

Heather looked the street up and down. There was a little light left in the sky, to the west, rimming above rooftops, chimneys cut black against it. Overhead, stars glistened, keeping their secrets. All was still, all was quiet.

She made for home.

CHAPTER TWENTY-ONE

It had begun to drizzle when Poppy pulled over the car. She took out her mobile phone from her bag in the passenger foot-well. She turned off the engine and sat for awhile, her phone in her lap. The rain gently pitter-pattered on the roof, the world smudged through the glass.

She looked at her phone and scrolled through the numbers. She found her uncle's number, her thumb hesitating over the screen. She shook her head, then scrolled into her favourites and dialled her husband. Once it connected, he picked up on the fourth ring.

"Hey, honey. You okay?" He sounded tired.

"Yes, I'm fine. Just checking in. How's Heather?"

"Good. She got a B on her English assignment."

"Martin…"

"What?"

"You do know I love you don't you?"

"Yes, but…"

"And you understand why I've had to come here?"

There was a pause. Static on the line. An entire ocean and a continent between them.

"Yes," he said, finally.

"I have to do this. I have to know."

"I know," he said, his voice low. Then: "Have you seen your uncle?"

"Not yet."

"Where are you staying?"

"I've got a room." This was a lie, but she didn't want him to fret.

"I'm fine."

"Okay. Well look…be safe. We're all good here, don't worry about us."

She pictured her house. Where Martin might be stood talking to her. He usually liked to pace the kitchen when on the phone, or his office. Thinking of her house tugged at her heart, the yearning part. Her life, her family, her world so very far away. She was back in this rainy, old country, on depressed streets of small, crumbling houses. Yet. There was another part of her—a long dormant part—that was reawakening. An ever stronger sense of belonging here, in this rainy, old land. It was in her blood, her being. A person's roots, she mused, can never leave you, no matter how far and how long you run from it.

"Poppy? You still there?"

"I'm here, Martin. I love you. I'll call again tomorrow."

"Okay, hon. Take care, love you."

She hung up. The rain was heavier now.

She put her phone back inside her bag then buttoned up her coat. She got out of the car and stepped onto Society Place.

***

Heather sat on her front step. It was early evening. The intense heat of the day was finally letting up; there was a cooling breeze. It had been so stifling during the mid-afternoon that sweat was running off her when she walked home from work. Tomorrow was Sunday, so off until Tuesday now. She planned to get stuff done around the house, to *take control* and make the place her own, as she was advised.

The house—and *all* its inhabitants—had been quiet for the past few nights, and Heather had slept, despite the heat. For once, the house felt calm, and still, and *hers*.

Down the other end of the street, a few kids sat on the curb in a huddle. Rafferty wasn't amongst them. A few cars drove past, but there was very little activity. Heather saw a young couple walking up the rise, hand in hand, leaning into one another, laughing, sunlight in their hair. It hurt her heart to look at them.

From her position on the front step, she could just about make out the edge of the school building further up the rise. The young couple walked past the school and she lost sight of them. She thought of her husband and of the baby in her tummy. She placed her hand flat on her stomach. "We're going to be alright," she said aloud. "Mummy loves you."

It was the first time she said those words to the little girl growing inside her. In her grief, in her shock, motherhood, the material impulse, had gotten lost. Lost in pain and sadness. But sitting there, on the front step of her house, on that summer's evening in 1976, Heather Lowes discovered the love inside her; an unconditional love, a bond, an impulse to protect and nurture. A mother's love, primal and natural and as ancient as mankind itself.

Above the rooftops the sun edged down the sky; TV aerials cut against its blood orange face.

***

Forty-three years later, Poppy Lowes, who kept her parents' name even after marrying Martin Levin in 2012, stood at the door of number 2, Society Place. The windows were all boarded up, as was the door. The next house was the same, and the one after that. An entire street boarded up. A condemned and forgotten place.

The wind scattered leaves along the street. The sky remained its slab of grey slate. There was no one around, save for the odd car. A dog barked somewhere far off.

Poppy lifted one foot and gently rested it on top of the step at the house's front door. She thought of her mother, pictured her from the photograph she carried in her purse. The only picture she had of both her parents together, so young and happy and free. Twenty years younger than Poppy was now. She took a look around, up and down the street, making sure there was no one about then she crouched down and gently ran her fingers over the stone step. She wiped her eyes and realised she was crying.

She turned to go when her phone rang. It made her jump. She pulled the phone from her bag and looked at the caller I.D. It was her uncle.

Poppy cleared her throat and answered the call.

"Poppy…"

"Hello, Michael." She knew she sounded shaky.

"Where are you?"

She frowned. "What do you mean?"

"I just spoke to Martin. He said you were here...in England...'

"Yes."

"Why didn't you..."

"I wanted to surprise you." She walked back to the car.

"Poppy..."

"Yes."

There was a pause. Poppy opened the car door, looking back at the house. There was crackling on the line. Then her uncle's voice came, low and full of concern.

"Poppy," he said. "I think I know what you're doing..."

Poppy waited.

Michael said, "Don't go to Society Place."

CHAPTER TWENTY-TWO

On the day the summer finally broke, Heather got up early. She hadn't slept well. The night had been stiflingly hot and she'd lay for hours sweating, the curtains and window open, the stars bright and abundant. No sound, no *sense*, came from the stairway beyond her door. Four nights now with no visits. The house was still.

She got out of bed at daybreak and went down to the kitchen and put the radio on. Thin Lizzy were doing *Rosalie*. Heather hummed along and opened the back door. She stepped out and looked at the sky. It was low, heavy, the clouds thick and black, the air was humid. It carried the scent of electricity. A storm was coming; the long, hot summer was about to break at last.

Heather went back inside and fixed herself some breakfast. The DJ was waffling on, reading letters sent in by listeners, but Heather hardly took any notice. It was just background noise. She put the kettle on the stove, then turned on the grill to make herself some toast. Michael had brought over some tools in a bucket the night before and had left them by the kitchen table. There was a large sponge and two scrapers of differing sizes. She planned to tackle the front room first.

She turned her toast over and Rod Stewart came on doing *Maggie May*. She sang along, stroking her belly. The kettle whistled and she made tea, then she froze.

She felt the thing watching her from the stairway opening.

She didn't turn around. Rod Stewart was still singing, her toast was burning. She noticed a gathering of ladybirds on her windowsill outside. She closed her eyes, then, without turning around, she said, "Not now."

Still it lingered.

A deep, low rumble of thunder moved through the sky. She sensed the thing cross the kitchen and come to stand behind her. The ladybirds were still there, out on the sill, moving up the glass. The low, heavy clouds gave the day a strange light, a half-light. Her toast caught alight and Heather moved fast, switching off the grill and blowing the flames away. The toast was charred, the smell strong. The thing was gone.

With a tea towel she got the toast out from under the grill and threw the pieces in the sink then she dowsed them with water from the tap. She looked out. The ladybirds were gone. Another low rumble cut across the sky. The air felt cooler all of a sudden and she smelt the rain coming. She turned the radio off and listened to the sky.

There was a flash of lightning. She looked to the ash tree and it scorched white against her retinas, leaving an after image. She counted to eight before there was a roll of thunder then the rain came, sudden and furious. The air smelt charged, metallic, electric. It smelt good.

She went to the back door and watched the storm. The air sent its first chill in months and her arms bristled. The rain was heavy and made a sharp, loud hissing sound. There were also thuds as it belted against her toilet roof. The sky was black; the thunderheads like billowing ink. Another fork of lightning, above the rooftops of Silver Hill Road, spidering down the sky. She counted five and then the crack of thunder came. This one very loud. A real window rattler.

Heather stepped out into the storm.

She was soaked in an instant. She came to stand in the middle of the yard and she watched the sky, holding her belly.

The rain was exhilarating. It was cold and hard, but felt purifying, cleansing. Lightning set the world in a blinding, piercing white moment, then thunder cracked right on its heel. The storm was on top of Society Place.

Heather looked up to the back of her house and saw the figure at the window. It was a tall man, faint in his image behind the glass and the strange light of the storm. But he was there and he was looking down at Heather. She didn't like his face. It didn't project any goodness whatsoever. As Rafferty had said, it was the face of a bad man.

Heather stepped back, until she was pressed up against the outhouse wall. She never took her eyes off him, and he, in turn, didn't take her eyes off her. Another fork of lightning heightened his image for a split second but in that small, fraction of time, Heather saw something hideous beneath the veneer of this man, this ghost. She saw its true form, its dead self. Decayed flesh hung from a skeletal frame, the loose skin rotten, blackened, eaten away.

Thunder boomed over the house, over Heather, over the dead man. The rain hissed. The ghost returned to its mask of hungry malevolence. Heather stepped forward and screamed at the shape in her window.

"This is my house! You do not get to control me…"

Her voice was small against the rain. Lightning forked right over her house, its crack loud, its tentacles burning an ephemeral imprint on the black clouds over the roof. The thunder came, more furious than before. She saw her window shake and the image of the ghost vibrate.

"GO AWAY!" she screamed. "I don't want you in my house. MY HOUSE!"

More lightning. More thunder. The height of the storm. More shifting in the appearance of the ghost, from decay to whole, from rotten flesh to stark white skin. Unnaturally white, ghostly white. Dead white.

Thunder again, lesser in its fury. Heather shouted again, but the intensity had left her. She now felt tired, and she was also now feeling the cold. Her hair was matted to her scalp and to her face; her clothes pasted to her skin. The fight was leaving her. The intensity of the rain was also dissipating. There came another flash of lightning, but this one was silent.

In the window, the ghost turned and *glided* from sight. The fear hit her then. The not seeing was scarier than seeing. She shook, from cold and from terror, and she waited. She looked through the kitchen window, to the opening of the stairway and waited for him to appear. And appear he did.

His feet came first, shoeless, naked, hovering an inch over each step, the legs rigid, dressed in grey. Then his entire form appeared at the opening, turning towards the kitchen. As soon as his face came into view, the eyes locked onto Heather. She remained rooted to the spot, the rain still falling, the sky still brooding.

The thing crossed the kitchen in an instant. Only its head moved, its body remained fixed, stone still. It arrived at the back door, the hungry eyes still locked onto Heather. There it gave pause, allowing Heather a brief moment to make sense of her thoughts. She wondered how this could be happening to her; how her life had turned so sour, so surreal. On one hand she was a pregnant widow who worked in a supermarket, and yet, on the other, she was a haunted person; haunted by grief and by an actual supernatural being, an entity of great malevolence. The thing looked at her with such hatred.

There was another lightning strike and two things happened at once. First the ghost rushed towards her. She screamed, but when the rain hit the entity, the drops seemed to rip through its form, tearing away a piece here, a piece there, a gash in his shoulder, a runny eye. Its head and face shredded in an instant. The second thing that happened was that a great fork of lightning struck the ash tree.

There was a loud crack and white flame burst in Heather's peripheral vision.

The ghost, in shreds and rags, almost reached Heather before the rain tore away the last of its image from reality. The crack caused Heather to turn and watch the great tree spark with light and fire. Then came the sound of splintering wood. Thunder rolled overhead and the tree groaned and cried out in cracks and breaks so loud they bounced off the surrounding houses. The great tree came down.

Heather instinctively backed up against the far wall. It fell towards the backyards of Society Place. The tree took its time, cracking and snapping all the way down. It spread itself across the gardens. Heather heard fences crushed beneath its weight; she heard glass smashing as Mr Newbold's greenhouse was totally destroyed. Gates were ripped from their hinges; a brick wall was toppled as the tree's great truck smashed into it. Great branches snapped, some spat up into the air and then came hurtling back down, one landed as close as Mrs Green's yard. Heather heard the thud against the dividing wall.

The great tree groaned and creaked and rustled as its expanse came to rest across several backyards. Once it was rested, the rain eased and the lightning ceased, as if the storm knew that its work here had been done.

The sky rumbled but it was distant, moving off.

Heather's legs finally gave out and she collapsed in a heap. She was cold, shivering, dazed. She could hear voices, back doors opening, the residents of the street all coming out to inspect the damage but these voices sounded far off. The world, and its realities of which Heather had lived in certainty, now seemed very far off. An echo of reality, for she now knew the truth of the world, and that truth was that there were layers.

Peel back the veneer of everyday life and you find a haunted world.

She heard somebody calling her name, but she was so fixed on her internal self that she failed to register the voice right away. Finally it cut into her thoughts simply because of the urgency of the tone. It was Mrs Green and she was shouting Heather's name over the wall. There was concern and fear in her tone.

Heather looked to the wall and saw the billow of white hair and two tiny eyes straining to see. "Heather..." she called. "Heather, are you alright my girl?"

Heather managed to say yes, but in truth, she wasn't sure she was alright. She hadn't been physically hurt by the storm, or the lightning struck tree, but she didn't feel right at all. Her world was upside down. She had glimpsed into a new world, another world. The world of the dead. She had seen a ghost with her own eyes. The rain had lacerated its materialism, its spirit, but she had seen it, had stared into his eyes and felt its hatred.

She managed to pick herself up, holding her belly as she did so. She staggered over to the wall and looked at Mrs Green's half obscured face and said, "Are you okay?"

"Yes, my dear. I'm fine. I think the tree has done a lot of damage though."

"Yes," said Heather, looking out to the thick and full branches that now rested against the earth.

"You should go and get dry," said Mrs Green. "You'll catch your death."

The phrase made Heather wince, but she said, "Yes...yes, I will," then without another word she headed back into the house.

CHAPTER TWENTY-THREE

Heather undressed in the kitchen and ran upstairs to dry herself down. Her bump was really showing now and she took a moment to admire it in the mirror. It was odd to see herself this way; she suspected most pregnant women must feel the same. Her body was no longer just her own. She now carried a human being within her. Her womb protected it. It grew inside her, feeding from her, connected to her in ways no other human being could ever be connected to her. She had been connected to her own mother in the same way and, in turn, the girl growing inside her would always be connected to her, no matter what. The tiny heart that beat within her, would, all being well, beat well into the next century, long past her own lifetime. Heather touched the wood surface of her bedside table to bless this thought.

Her breasts were larger, filling with milk, readying to feed the baby. Her body was her own; it wasn't sexualised in its nakedness. It was beautiful in its giving and nurturing of life.

She turned from the mirror and redressed in an old t-shirt and shorts. Outside, the rain had eased considerably. Now it fell steadily, lightly tapping at the bedroom window. She lay on the bed and curled into a foetal position, imagining her baby doing the same inside her. She stared at the window, at the dark sky beyond her flapping curtains. Now the storm had moved on, the heat in the day had returned. She held her belly and wondered about her daughter, trying to imagine what she'd look like, how she'd be, what her personality would be like; she imagined her walking and talking and laughing and making friends and going to school and crying and hurting and how she'd hold her and tell her that everything was going to be alright; she thought of her daughter growing into adulthood, she wondered if she'd live long enough to see her get married and have children of her own. She wondered how far into the new millennium her daughter's heart would beat for. She imagined numbers, years, 2020, 2035, 2040, times that seemed so impossibly far away.

She watched the curtains moving and the heavy sky and she drifted off to sleep. She dreamed that her daughter was all grown up and was stood outside number 2, Society Place. In the dream, her daughter was crying.

CHAPTER TWENTY-FOUR

Mr Newbold lived alone. Always had, always would. His Christian name was Arthur but everyone addressed him as Mr Newbold. He doubted many people even knew his Christian name. He certainly carried the air of someone known so formally. He was stern, headmasterly, but not without humour. It was a dry humour mind, so dry most people mistook it for rudeness. Mainly though, he kept himself to himself. He liked being alone. Alone in the sense of another living person co-habiting his house anyway. He wasn't totally alone.

After the storm had died down he went out back to inspect the damage. It was worse than he'd imagined. The greenhouse was gone, completely crushed. He couldn't even see it beneath the wreckage of the tree. Branches and foliage had overtaken the yard. He could just make out his back fence, which had been split in two, and bricks around his raised flowered bed had been knocked out, soil and plants spilling out into the yard. He wanted to cry, to rage, but he held it back. He was a restrained man, and it wouldn't do to let go now. There would be time for that later. He looked to the sky. It was still dark, brooding, ominous, and the distant sound of thunder came and went with the breeze.

He went back inside and found that his table and chair turned over, the legs sticking up, and all his cupboard doors open. Angry and upset by the damage the tree had caused, he was in no mood for games.

"That's enough, Simon," he said. "Not today, thank you."

He busied himself righting the table and chair, muttering to himself. He needed a brandy and a sit down.

Something hit him on the back of the neck. It was wet.

He flinched and span around. The cupboard doors were closed. A wet tea towel lay on the floor. He put his hand to the back of his neck, wiping the moister away.

"Simon!" he said. He bent down to pick up the towel when a cup shot across the kitchen, narrowly missing Mr Newbold's head, smashing against the far wall. Newbold screamed and fell to the floor, backing up against the table.

"Simon?" he asked, his voice low. This was new. In all the time Mr Newbold had known about the ghost in his house, he had never felt afraid. Not truly afraid. Simon, as Mr Newbold had come to call the spirit, had been more of a trickster, a hider of keys, a banger of doors, nothing more than that. Simon had never physically connected with Mr Newbold and had certainly never thrown anything at him before.

"Simon?" Mr Newbold said again. All was quiet. Outside there came another distant rumble of thunder and the wet sounds of a world shaking off the storm. Newbold looked to his kitchen shelf full of cups and glasses. He stood up slowly.

A tea cup with a flowery pattern shot straight towards him. Mr Newbold ducked and the cup smashed against the wall behind him. Then another came. He noticed this one a little too late and it hit him on the shoulder. He yelped and the cup fell to his feet, smashing on impact. Then a glass came and caught him just above his right eye. It didn't smash, but left a nasty mark. Mr Newbold fell back against the table then cups and glasses, saucers and salt shakers all flew across the kitchen. Most of these connected with Mr Newbold. Some of these bounced off him, leaving bruises, while others did smash, cutting him, drawing blood.

Mr Newbold fell to the floor and curled into a foetal position, covering his head against the onslaught. Once the cups and glasses were exhausted, the cupboard fell open and plates and crockery began to hurtle towards Mr Newbold. The noise was terrific. He kept his eyes closed hoping to God it would end soon.

It didn't.

Soon the knives and forks came out and began to slash and pierce into his flesh. After a while he stopped screaming. He had no scream left. The pain and the fear were all too great.

Once his heart gave out and his life slipped from his body, then, and only then, did the poltergeist stop.

CHAPTER TWENTY-FIVE

When Heather woke it was the afternoon and there was a lot of noise coming from outside. She got up and went to the front window. There was an ambulance and a fire engine blocking the street and many people about, uniformed and resident. She wondered if the tree had hurt somebody when it came down, then thought about going out and seeing if she could help in anyway (or just to see what the hell was going on), but then the image of the shape at the window came to her and that put fire in her belly.

She went downstairs, got a glass of water from the tap and looked out at the felled tree across the backyards as she drank then she set to work. She ran the hot tap and filled Michael's bucket up then she took the scraper into the front room. She flicked the TV on for company then set to work. She dowsed the walls with the wet sponge and she began to scrape at the wallpaper.

Pebble Mill at One was on the television. They were interviewing Doris Stokes but the volume was low and Heather hardly paid it any mind. It was just background noise. The back door was open still and she could hear voices out in the yards but she remained at her work. She wanted everything in the house stripped back. She was going to start again, decorate the entire place so nothing remained from before she moved in. She was taking back the house, making it her own.

In places, there seemed to be two or three layers of wallpaper, and it was a struggle at first. She dug the scraper in, but only managed to tear away a small strip of paper. On top was an orangey-brown patterned wallpaper, beneath that seemed to be a green flowery one and the final layer appeared to be a black, white and pale blue mosaic. Once she'd gotten a few pieces stripped away, she had more of a chance of getting the scraper right under, flat against the plaster, and began to strip away larger and larger strips.

It was tough going but Heather didn't slow, she kept on at it until she had a good section of the wall exposed.

Pebble Mill had finished now and there was cricket on, the echoey thump of bat and ball and systematic cheering and clapping soothed her, yet she didn't once look at the screen. Her focus remained fixed on her scraper and paper it peeled. She didn't even register the markings at first, not on the surface anyway.

She worked for hours, pulling larger and larger strips off the wall until the floor was cover in torn and shredded wallpaper and the light had shifted and darkened outside. On the walls was horsehair plaster, strong stuff, and drawn or scratched into the plaster were markings and symbols the likes of which Heather had never before seen. There were a great many circles, circles within circles, stars, crosses, holy and otherwise, and a great many eyes.

She stood back and stared at the walls. The thud of bat and ball registering somewhere in the distance.

***

Chloe was startled by a banging on the front door. She was washing clothes in the sink. The great felled tree was through her kitchen window, her back fence completely destroyed. Rafferty had seen the entire thing from his bedroom and now refused to come downstairs. He had already been quiet and unresponsive and the storm and the tree had not helped his fragile mind. Chloe hadn't the strength to deal with him. Not today. She was washing clothes in an effort to take her mind off the tragic death of Mr Newbold. She was in a state of shock.

Chloe had heard the noise coming from next door and had gone out into the garden to call him. The destroyed fence meant there was access into his yard, although she'd had to traverse the debris of the tree.

She'd found Mr Newbold dead on his kitchen floor. The kitchen looked as if the lightning storm had struck it. The entire place had been upturned. There were broken crockery and glasses and lord knows what else all across the floor. Mr Newbold had forks sticking out of his legs and arms. Chloe had thrown up then scrambled back home to call an ambulance. They came within twenty minutes.

Chloe had stayed at home awhile the paramedics registered the death and examined the body. The police arrived soon after, and a coroner had been called, but still hadn't arrived. The police and ambulance service left, meaning that Mr Newbold was still on the kitchen floor, covered over no doubt, but still there, waiting for the coroner to come a pick him up, and Chloe couldn't stand the thought of him still in there, in the wrecked kitchen, dead on the floor of the house he'd lived in for thirty-odd years. It was an unbearable thought and now someone was banging on her front door.

"Yes! Alright!" she shouted then dried her hands on a tea-towel and crossed the kitchen, into the front room, and opened the door to see a very stricken Heather Lowes stood out on the pavement.

"Can you come?" she said.

"Well, Rafferty's upstairs…"

"Please…just for a minute. I need you to see something."

Chloe looked back into the house then said, "Okay, if we're quick," then she left, closing the front door behind her.

***

Chloe knew what the markings were as soon as she walked into Heather's house. She knew because she had seen them in her own house, on her own walls. Heather's television was on and her floor was covered in paper. Heather herself looked tired and hot.

Chloe said, "Are you alright?"

Heather looked at her. Chloe didn't think she was going to answer but then she said, very quietly, "Yes," but offered no more.

"You should sit down."

"I'm fine," she said, but sounded far from it. "What are these things are all over my walls?"

Chloe hesitated then said, "They are apotropaic marks."

Heather stared at her. Chloe continued. "They are supposed to ward off evil spirits."

Heather laughed. Chloe pointed to one of the eye symbols. "These are Nazar. Eyes are often used to ward off the evil eye and here..." she pointed to hideous face up in the corner above the opening to the kitchen, up by the architrave. "This is a Grotesquerie. They are used around windows and doorways that are particularly vulnerable to the entry or passage of evil."

"Of evil?" said Heather, her eyes watering.

"Yes."

Heather looked around the room, running her hands through her hair.

"Heather..."

Heather turned her attention to Chloe.

"Heather. There's something you should know..."

"What is it?"

"Mr Newbold died this afternoon."

Heather blinked, unsure how to take this news. She hadn't known the man and wasn't sure what to say or what to feel.

"I believe..." said Chloe, "...I believe that the spirit that inhabited his house, a spirit that Mr Newbold called Simon...well, I...I believe Simon killed Mr Newbold."

Heather continued staring at Chloe. Finally she said, "What should I do?"

"Do you want the honest answer?"

"Yes."

Chloe bit her top lip, then said, "I believe you should leave this house now...before it's too late."

***

Rafferty lay in his bed. His eyes wide open. The girl had been stood at the end of his bed since his mother left the house. He was too petrified to move.

The girl had her teeth bared, her eyes wide. Her skin was translucent. She stood stone still, her face fixed in terror.

Rafferty felt himself wee the bed again, but he couldn't move.

PART THREE
1976/2019

CHAPTER TWENTY-SIX

Michael Grant lived in a converted barn up in Derbyshire, near a place called Whatstandwell. Poppy had always liked the name, but had never actually visited Michael's place. He'd lived there for about eight years, and Poppy hadn't set foot on English soil for over a decade. He'd sent her photos and postcards over the years and driving through Whatstandwell it was as she imagined. Earthy, rocky, English. It brought to mind men working down pits and pints down the legion and women in pinafore aprons gossiping over garden walls. Michael lived up a narrow road, surrounded by fields and a view of the village of Whatstandwell below.

As Poppy approached the barn house—a place that to Poppy's mind looked cold and damp and lonely—her uncle came out of the front door, waved and waited. She pulled up, gravel crunching under the tyres, and got out. Michael approached her. He looked very old and very gaunt but then he was seventy years old. He wore a tatty old fisherman's jumper, brown corduroys and tartan slippers. He looked unwashed and unhealthy. Yet, it amused Poppy somewhat to see this epitome of a Derbyshire man. Back home in the States, a lot of the men she knew around her uncle's age didn't look nearly as old as her uncle did. Her husband's father was still running 10ks and boating on Lake Tahoe, her uncle on the other hand looked like he might have trouble walking down to the village.

"Poppy," he said as he reached her, her arms open, his smile warm.

"Hello Uncle," she said, falling into his embrace. They held each for a long time. He felt tiny in her arms and smelt fusty. Looking over his shoulder, out to the fields beyond his barn, Poppy thought how brutal the winters must be up here.

She pulled away and looked at him. "It's so lovely to see you."

"And you," he said. His voice was croaky. It warbled. "Let's go inside. I'll put the kettle on."

***

Inside, the barn was indeed cold, despite the fire crackling away in the main room. The place smelt like her uncle, fusty, unclean, old, and there were newspapers and books everywhere, piled up, spilling across the floor. There was a TV set that looked like something from another time and rugs and throws over the settee and the chair by the fireside. All, she suspected, to battle the bitter cold this place must see. There was also an acoustic guitar in one corner of the room. That too was dusty.

Michael attempted to straighten out the ball of throws on the settee and then said, "Please, sit down, I'll make the tea."

"Thank you," she said and perched herself on the edge.

"Your accent is stronger than when I last saw you," he said.

"Transatlantic drawl. Martin still thinks I sound really English but over here I know I sound American. There are certain words that catch me out, I suppose..."

"I like it." He shuffled off into the kitchen and Poppy could hear him banging and clattering about.

She stood up and moved around the room. There was a dusty old record player to the side of the fireplace. It sat on top of a table, below which was a stack of vinyl. Poppy crouched down and went through them. Wishbone Ash, Pink Floyd, The Groundhogs, Black Sabbath, Jimi Hendrix, Mike Oldfield: names and record sleeves that triggered childhood memories. She would have played some of these very records in her girlhood. She pulled out *Ziggy Stardust and the Spiders From Mars*. She knew this one very well. She used to play it all the time. Mainly because her uncle had told her that it had belonged to her mother.

Michael came through with two cups of tea.

"You've found the records then."

"Yes," said Poppy, standing and taking the tea from her uncle. She went and sat back down on the settee. Michael took the chair by the fire. They sipped from their mugs and listened to the fire popping and crackling.

Finally, Poppy said, "How are you, Michael?"

"Oh, you know, mustn't grumble."

"How long have you been up here? Eight years?"

"Nine."

"Wow, that long…"

"Why didn't you tell me you were coming over?"

Poppy didn't answer at first.

Michael answered for her. "You came to go to the house, didn't you?"

"No…I…"

"You mustn't go there. It's not safe for you."

"But…I have to know…"

"No, you don't."

"But it's my daughter, Michael…"

"Is Heather okay?"

"Yes, but…she's…she's begun to see things."

Michael put his cup down on the arm of his chair. "What things?"

Poppy swallowed then said, "My mother."

CHAPTER TWENTY-SEVEN

Michael lay on his bed listening to Mike Oldfield's *Hergest Ridge*. He played the record a lot. He preferred it to *Tubular Bells*. He liked *Ommadawn* as well, but *Hergest Ridge* was his favourite. He found it to be the most emotional of the three records, and he loved Oldfield's guitar playing.

He closed his eyes. Rain was falling outside. It was heavy. Summer seemed a long time ago.

The girl at his side was still asleep. He lit up a joint and lost himself in the music. He imagined himself recording an album like *Hergest Ridge*. Holed up in a studio somewhere, laying down different instruments, creating vast soundscapes with guitars and keyboards and whatever else he could get his hands on; music to move you, to take you somewhere. Something like Oldfield's work, or the Floyd, or Genesis. That was the dream.

The girl stirred next to him. He'd met her in Talk of the Midlands the night before. Her name was Annabel and she loved Led Zeppelin and was interested in horoscopes, tarot cards and astral projection, but that was all he knew about her. After the club they'd walked back to his, played records, drank wine, got stoned then fucked like only strangers can fuck. They didn't get to sleep until dawn, now it was midday and Annabel was only just waking.

She opened her eyes and looked at him, then became conscious of where she was and who she was with. She also realised she was naked and pulled the covers up over her.

"Hey," said Michael.

"Hey," she returned.

Michael leaned across to the record player and turned it down a little. The rain outside became more noticeable. It was really hammering it down.

"You want a drink?" he asked her.

"Water...please."

He went over to his kitchen and took out a glass. He noticed that Annabel used this moment to quickly put on her bra and t-shirt. Once her top half was covered, she riffled around on the floor looking for her underwear. Michael turned his back to her, pretending to get something from one of the cupboards to allow her some privacy. He filled the glass with water from the tap then took it over to her. She was now dressed in her jeans and was stood up. She thanked him for the water and drank the lot in one.

"I needed that. My mouth is so dry."

"That'll be all the wine," he said.

"Yes...we certainly had a session. And on a school night as well."

He laughed.

"What time is it?" she asked.

"Gone twelve."

"Jesus. What time did we...erm...get to sleep?"

"I don't know, but the sun was coming up."

The first side of *Hergest Ridge* came to an end, so Michael went over and turned the record over, carefully dropping the needle in the groove.

"I should be going?" said Annabel.

"You can stay...if you like? You want some food?"

"No, I should get back. Feed the cat, take a shower, y'know?"

"Sure."

"Cool."

Neither of them moved. They looked at each other and the awkwardness of the situation caused them both to laugh.

"Well..." began Annabel. "We've seen each other naked and exchanged bodily fluids and are now incapable of speaking to one another."

She said this in good humour and it put them both at ease.

"You wanna cup of tea? Get to know each other..."

"I think we got to know each other pretty well last night...or this morning...whichever way you wanna look at it..."

"No, I mean...get to know each other properly."

She laughed, "I know what you mean. Like, what do I do, where do I live, what's my favourite band, that kind of thing?"

"Yes."

"Well I think I'm going to go and retain some mystery."

Michael smiled. He liked this girl.

"Okay, well if I could call you..."

She smiled. "You don't have to say that."

"No, no, I want to...I...I'd like to see you again."

She went over and kissed him. There was something different about this girl.

Her lips left his and she said, "Gotta pen?"

CHAPTER TWENTY-EIGHT

Come rain or shine, the children of St Chad's school were sent out into the playground at dinnertime. Rafferty watched the other children from inside the hood of his parka coat. His arm was on the mend. It was no longer in a sling, but remained in plaster.

Out in the yard, most of the kids were tear-arsing around and farting about the way kids do. Girls stood in huddles, under umbrellas, boys racing around, many of them with their coats undone to show how hard they were. The rain had steadied to a drizzle but Rafferty's coat was still slick with water. He stood at the far end of the playground. Behind was the dungeon. This was what the children called the dark space beneath the school; the place out of bounds for pupils. A great many kids ignored this rule, however. Teachers were forever chasing children out from under there. It was blocked off by a high tensile fence, but there were plenty of gaps, plenty of ways to get in and out. It was mainly boys that were caught sneaking down there but from time to time the odd girl was caught by curiosity, or, in the case of Sally Flynn, took down there by two older boys who scared her out of her wits by pretending to be monsters, chasing her around in the dark. Rafferty liked Sally Flynn and had felt bad for her. He didn't like her as much as he liked Becky Philips, but she was definitely second best.

However, girls weren't really on Rafferty's mind on that rainy early October day in 1976. Not living girls anyway.

Since going back to school, Rafferty had felt detached. Truth be told, he'd felt detached for some time, but being back at school had exacerbated the feeling. Being surrounded by all the other kids just confounded how alone and unreal he felt. He'd taken to speaking very little, something that had been picked up on by teachers and kids alike. His mother had noticed the change in him also (but, Raff had noted, she seemed distant herself). Everyone had noticed the change in him, everyone aside from his dad that is, who was oblivious to most things.

Something made him turn around.

He stared into the darkness of the dungeon, his back to the playground. The parka's hood obscured his peripheral vision, so he could only see what was right in front of him. Through the fence, in the dark, by one of the pillars, there was a shape.

"*Hey,*" it said. "*Come here, kid.*"

The voice, low, guttural, male, frightened Rafferty very badly. The playground behind him seemed to fade away; his ears tuned into the direction of the voice.

"*Kid, come 'ere.*"

Before Rafferty registered what he was doing, he was crawling through a gap in the fencing—one of the many gaps that pupils slipped through all the time. Rafferty, however, had only crawled through to the dungeon once before. Lee Cope had dared him to go down there and he doubled-dared back, but then Lee Cope had tripled-dared him so he'd had to do it, and he'd got caught by Mr Johns and got a lunchtime detention for his trouble. He'd never done it again.

But now he was through and into the dark once more. He could just make out the shape stood behind the pillar. It was tall, with a long, bony finger beckoning him forward. Rafferty knew that he should be running away, telling teacher, never setting foot in the dungeon again, but something was pulling him forward. His eyes were transfixed on the beckoning hand, those long, bony talons; he felt mesmerised by the shape under the school, in the dark.

"*Come 'ere, I've got something for you...*" it said.

Rafferty managed to tear his eyes away, for a brief moment, to glance back at the world he was leaving behind. Children were playing, laughing, running, hop-scotching in the bright autumn daylight. Beneath the school, it was cold. It smelt funny. Everything was telling Rafferty to run but he could not.

"*That's it,*" the voice said. "*Keep coming.*" The finger beckoned.

With every step, Rafferty's mind fogged over. His inner darkened, until he no longer thought about the kid's playing behind him, his school, his mother, his life. These things ebbed away as the finger kept beckoning.

Shafts of light splintered in from the metal grates on the far wall. These being at pavement level out at the front of the school,

Rafferty saw the wheels of a vehicle pass by on the road. He heard its sound, registered that it belonged to the ordinary world, the real world. Down here however, in the dark, reality was slipping with every step.

"*That's it, boy*," the shape said. "*Come along. The nest awaits.*"

Rafferty reached the shape and took its hand. Part of him knew that this was a very wrong thing to do but his body did it for him. He felt a little like he had after his fall from the tree in the summer. In the ambulance, the pain had been so great that he swam in and out of consciousness. He hadn't been sure what was real and what was in his mind.

The fingers were long and scaly. They looked brittle but the grip was firm.

Rafferty looked up into the eyes of the thing in the dark. It was a man, or something that was once a man. The same scaly, brittle looking skin hung from his face. His eyes glistened, caught by the light coming through the metal grates. His mouth was black. It appeared to drip darkness, like runny tar was spilling from its black and crooked teeth.

It spoke. "*We've been told about you, boy.*" It smiled, more darkness running from its mouth.

Inside Rafferty's head, he was screaming, but the scream wouldn't come from his head to his mouth. His throat was blocked.

The fingers wrapped around his wrist—his plastered wrist—and pulled at him, and Rafferty felt himself being dragged along the dungeon floor. He thought of the shape as a Once-Man.

The name fixed firmly in his mind, along with the scream that grew louder and louder. He glanced to the playground. Somewhere far off, he heard the school whistle and children were lining up ready to go back inside.

"*Come*," said the Once-Man, dragging him ever deeper into the dark.

Rafferty only began to struggle when he saw the hole. It was similar in size to the hole in Mrs Lowes' cellar, but this one emanated an even more terrible smell. Rafferty coughed and gagged when the smell hit his nose. It seemed to awaken all his senses because suddenly he could struggle and kick and fight. He also found his voice and began to scream. He screamed for help, for his mother, for his teacher, for anybody, but nobody came.

"*Come!*" The Once-Man pulled him into the hole.

Rafferty fought with everything he had. He clawed at the Once-Man, kicked, spat, but its grip remained like a vice. Part of Rafferty registered the pain flare up beneath the plaster on his arm, but the fear, the struggle, the rancid smell, all of these things allowed the pain to be something only half felt and half understood.

As he was pulled into the hole, his fingers scratched at the brick wall. He felt the warm blood run down his good arm.

"*Come down with us*," said the Once-Man and then Rafferty was snatched from the world.

CHAPTER TWENTY-NINE

It was approaching 3p.m. and the end of Heather's shift. She'd been sat at the till for two hours straight and it'd been busy; she now needed rest. She'd been getting stomach pains throughout the day and her right foot felt funny—a dull ache. In the brief moments of pause between customers, Heather had sat and watched the rain outside. Her till faced the large shop windows and she could see out to the car park. Maggie tried to engage her in conversation, but she had grown weary of the woman. Heather had found that Maggie was a gossip and not very nice with it. Carol, on the other hand, who existed under the illusion of power, had realised that Heather couldn't be intimidated by her and thus, left her alone. She still gave Maggie and a few of the others a hard time but with Heather she kept her distance. Heather for her part, kept herself to herself. She did her shift, was pleasant to the customers (even the unpleasant ones), and then went home. Maggie had invited her to the pub one afternoon and had taken it as a personal affront when Heather turned her down. Heather had wanted to remind her she was nearly eight months pregnant and a widow—as if it wasn't blatantly obvious—and to ask her what possible lure would an afternoon in a smoky pub hold for her, but she didn't.

Between customers again, Heather gazed out of the window. The rain had slowed, the sky low and grey. Autumn had definitely set in. The leaves were turning, falling, scattering down pavements, the long hot summer finally at an end. Heather was glad it was over.

She looked at her watch. Five minutes left of her shift. A man approached her till. Heather smiled but inside she felt a wave of unease fill her. Something about the man felt off, wrong. He was in his mid-thirties perhaps, or early forties, and rail thin, ugly thin. He had no hair on his head. He was completely smooth. Even his eyebrows were gone.

He had no items to purchase, yet he came to stand in front of Heather's till. His clothes were filthy; his fingernails long and black. Heather felt her heart thumping against her chest. She looked over the man's shoulder to Maggie, but Maggie was serving somebody and had her back to Heather. She looked about her. There was only her and Maggie manning the tills, not even Carol was about.

The man smiled. His teeth were disgusting. "Hello, little girl…"

Terror rattled through Heather when she realised the man wasn't addressing her.

The man was talking to her belly.

Heather couldn't move. The man reached out and placed his palm onto her bump. She whimpered and felt a tear slip from her eye.

"Lovely," said the man, then he pulled his hand away and slowly brought his eyes up to meet Heathers. "And hello to you, too." His smile faded.

Somewhere in the distance, Heather could hear Maggie talking away to her customer but it was remote, like voices heard through a wall.

"Do you speak?" he asked her. His breath was repulsive.

"Yes," she said in little more than a whisper.

"You live in my house."

Heather looked at him, stunned, then said, "Shaw?"

The man smiled. There was no warmth to it.

"You've discovered things in my house, haven't you?"

Heather swallowed, blinked the water from her eyes, and said, "It's my house now."

Shaw laughed. It was guttural. "No, Mrs Lowes, you're just keeping it warm for us."

"What...?" she began, but couldn't finish.

"Go on."

"What did you leave in my house?"

Shaw slowly swept his hand over his bald head. "You have got the wrong impression of me, my dear. I didn't *leave* anything there. Nothing that I conjured anyway. The things in that house...on that street...were already there. I just gave them a little encouragement is all."

"What is it?"

"It's not an *it*, Mrs Lowes, it's a *them*. There is a nest of ghosts on Society Place. Always has been. I don't know, they might have been there before there were even buildings on that hill of land."

"A nest of ghosts?"

"Yes, Mrs Lowes, and I think..." He leaned forward so that his face was inches from her own. "...they've taken a shine to you. And your baby."

That is when Heather began to scream. She screamed at Shaw to GET OUT, screamed it over and over again. Maggie and her customer looked round in horror. Carol came running down an aisle. Shaw fled from the store and was gone before Carol or Maggie reached her.

Heather collapsed into hysteria. Both Maggie and Carol looking frightened, not knowing what to do. Heather griped her belly and cried. A gut-wrenching, outpouring of pain and fear and anger.

Maggie tried to touch her, but Heather raged, knocking her away.

Mr Sullivan came rushing down the aisle then and looked as stricken as the others. They all stood around, letting Heather cry her heart out.

Finally exhaustion overcame her and she fell into Maggie's arms and sobbed into her hair. Maggie held her, stroking her back, letting the last shudders of Heather's pain escape her.

Once Heather had calmed, they fussed. They wanted to know if the man had assaulted her, they wanted to call the police, call an ambulance, call Heather's brother. They wanted to make sure she was alright, that the baby was fine; all these things, all these questions, they were all too much for Heather.

Finally, she picked herself up and walked out. They let her go. They were too stunned to do anything else.

CHAPTER THIRTY

Heather didn't want to go home. The thought of stepping back into that—
nest of ghosts
—house was unbearable. She thought about going to Tom and Jean's house, asking if she could move back in, but she hadn't seen them for weeks. They seemed to have distanced themselves from her completely. Perhaps she just reminded them of their son, and the life he could be living, and they just didn't want to be reminded at all. Heather could understand that. Either way, they seemed to have slipped from Heather's life. Perhaps it would be different after the baby was born, but for now they seemed to have made it clear she was on her own.

Instead of Tom and Jean's, she headed for her brother's flat, not expecting to stay—you couldn't swing a cat in his place—but just to see him. She hadn't seen much of him for the past several weeks, not since he did all the work in the cellar, but she knew he was busy with his band and with his job. It would be good for her to see him.

***

A very pretty girl answered Michael's door. 10CC's *I'm Mandy Fly Me* was playing inside the flat. The sight of the girl put Heather on the back foot.

"Hello?" said the girl. She was wearing one of Michael's t-shirts—Heather recognised it—which fell over her like a dress. Her legs were bare.

"Hi…" said Heather, her voice sounding very small to her ears. "Is Michael there?"

"Err, no, he's at work."

"Oh."

The girl narrowed her eyes at Heather. "Can I give him a message?"

Heather bit back tears. She said, "No," and turned and left.

She heard the girl close the flat door. She didn't look back.

***

Heather sat in the park, the trees shaking off the rain. The bench was wet, dampening her behind, but still she sat. She didn't have the strength to get up. The wind moved through the branches, a dog chased a ball, the city hummed beyond the green. She tried to remember who she was. Tried to the remember the girl she was, the family she once had, the childhood home, the school she went to, the friends she had had, but all of it was cloudy, like a half remembered dream.

She tried to remember the husband she'd had, for that brief snatch of time, but he was hazy too. She thought of ghosts, and thought of herself as a ghost, a half person, a shell where once a woman lived, a woman who laughed and loved and cried and felt love, and was loved. She could barely remember that person either.

Heather ran a hand over her belly, over the living being growing inside her, the girl she would call Poppy, after the affectionate name her father had once given her little girl self, the name her brother adopted after their father's death, which he used in moments of tenderness. The girl inside her who would grow and live into the next century, the beating heart that would beat long into an age she will never know. She was sure of this now.

She sat, inside herself. Sat on that wet bench feeling alone and unreal. The loneliness was a void, a black maw, wanting to swallow her whole.

The wind kicked up, rustling through the trees. A dog was barking.

"Anthony," she said. "Why did you leave me?"

She looked to the grey sky as she said this, because that's what humans do.

***

She headed back to Society Place. There was nowhere else to go.

She took the rise, walking down to the school. There was a police car outside the school and a group of people huddled on the pavement. Heather heard the crying from quite a distance. It was a wailing, a cry of immense agony. As she got closer Heather saw that the person in such great distress was Chloe. A police officer was holding her fast and Chloe was screaming at a woman across from her, "WHERE'S MY SON? WHERE IS MY BOY?" over and over again. The woman across from her was also crying, shaking her head, looking stunned and frightened and guilty.

Heather picked up speed and burst in on the scene, grabbing her friend and embracing her. Chloe looked into Heather's eyes and said, "My boy...my beautiful boy is missing." She sobbed, snot and tears and haunted eyes, then she screamed, "MY BOY IS GONE."

Heather pulled Chloe into her, stroking her hair, letting the woman break down and shudder against her.

The teacher—the Head, Heather presumed—looked utterly stricken; she looked about ready to fall to the curb. The police officers, two of them, looked young and unsure of what to do or what to say.

Chloe shook in her arms and Heather wondered what kind of terrible, terrible place they all lived in. These old houses, slates dark with rain, stacked in rows, filled with families, harbouring a nest of ghosts.

CHAPTER THIRTY-ONE

"A woman came around for you," said Annabel. She was watching Michael closely to see how he responded, and he responded in much the way she imagined he would—a furrowed brow, a flash of guilt as he tried to work out who it could have been, then a mask of control.

"Who was it?" he said. He put his guitar case against the wall and took his coat off.

"She didn't say, but she really seemed to want to see you. She was pretty, dark hair...*pregnant*." She really emphasized the word pregnant.

Michael laughed. He looked relieved. Now it was Annabel's turn to furrow her brow.

"That's my sister," he said. "Heather."

"Oh," said Annabel.

"Did she seem okay?"

"Well...she seemed a little distressed to be honest."

"And you didn't let her in?"

She didn't like the way he said this. "She didn't give me a chance. As soon as she found out you weren't in she just took off."

Michael started to put his coat back on and collect up his keys. "I'd better go and see her."

"Why didn't you tell me you had a sister? A pregnant sister at that?"

"I don't know," he said, distracted. "I guess...I guess we've been having such a good time I didn't want to get into everything."

She sat on the end of the bed. "I suppose we haven't really told one another much about our actual lives."

"No...but...maybe we should, y'know...if this..."

"If this...?"

"If this is becoming a thing."

"A thing?"

"Yeah, a thing."

She got up and walked over to him.

"Do you want it to become a thing?" she asked.

He smiled and moved closer to her. "Do you?"

"I don't know...I'll have to think about it."

***

Annabel went with him to Society Place. The van was being a bit temperamental and took a few turns of the key before the engine fired up, but once they were going it was fine, and it was only a short journey to Heather's. Annabel asked him about his sister and in two double blows learned that their parents had died in a car crash, and so had Heather's husband, of only a few months. Michael said these things matter-of-factly but she could tell he was hiding a lot of pain and grief.

He told her that he felt bad for not seeing Heather much in recent weeks. He blamed it on how busy he'd been with the band but Annabel knew that it wasn't just his music that had been occupying him and she felt pangs of guilt. He knew it too, but was good enough not to mention their days in bed as a factor in Michael's absence from his sister's life.

When they got to Society Place the street was quiet. Not a soul about.

He pulled up outside number 2 and turned off the engine. He leaned over his steering wheel and looked at the house. He looked worried.

They both got out the van and went to the front door. Michael looked the street up and down then knocked.

No one came to the door.

He knocked several more times, looking increasingly agitated and concerned.

"Come on," he said through his teeth, then knocked again, really banging on the door.

Annabel sensed that there was more to his concern than he was letting on, something he hadn't told her, but she remained quiet. After another rap on the door, Michael pulled out his keys and picked through them.

"Do you have a key?" asked Annabel.

"Yes. I'm gonna have a check inside...make sure she's not in there."

"Yes." She was unsure if she should stay out on the street or if he wanted her to go in with her.

He found the key, slid it into the lock, then pushed the door inwards. They both stood out on the pavement, peering in.

The walls were covered in markings. Strips of wallpaper covered the carpet. Furniture was over turned; the chair in front of the telly was on its side. The small coffee table was in the centre of the room, its legs in the air. There was a smell too—a smell of rotten eggs. Annabel held her hand to her nose.

Michael glanced at her. He looked outright frightened now.

Michael stepped into the house and Annabel followed.

They both looked at the walls, at the markings, the strange, unnerving shapes and symbols. Annabel gently closed the front door behind her and immediately wished she hadn't. Michael looked at her but didn't say anything. He looked stricken.

He moved through the room, past the cellar door, and into the kitchen. Annabel quickly followed him.

It was dark in the kitchen. The blinds were down, and it was cold. Very cold. Too cold. Annabel hugged herself and commented on the temperature but Michael didn't answer her. He was staring at the windows, a confused expression on his face. "This isn't right," he muttered then took a step further into the room. Annabel did the same and that's when she noticed that the blinds were moving. *Pulsing*, that was the word that entered her head. Her eyes reconfigured, altering the signals in the brain from what she *thought* she was looking at—blinds—to what she *actually* was looking at: Hundreds, perhaps thousands, of tiny insects, all crawling over on another, a mass pulse of ladybirds.

She screwed up her face. "What the hell..."

Michael rushed over to the back door and unlocked it, swinging it open. The ladybirds took flight, swarming the kitchen. Annabel screamed as they landed on her. Ten, twenty, fifty, covering her coat, her face, her hair, all in a matter of moments. Except it didn't feel like moments. It felt like a long time. She could hear them fluttering about her ears, felt them crawling about in her ears, her neck; they scurried up into her hair. In the involuntary reaction of opening her mouth and screaming, several flew down her windpipe, causing her to choke, cough, spit, wretch. She battered her head and face with her hands. Squeezing her eyes shut, hearing the hard shells of the insects crushed under her assault, feeling them mashed on her palms.

More and more ladybirds came. She felt their weight on her, the mass clumps of moving, scuttling creatures, spreading across her body. She felt them on her legs, her arms, her back. She heard them. They were in her ears, over her eyes, up her nose. She fell to the floor and writhed around until she could take it no longer and let loose an unbridled scream; a scream from the core, from where the fear lives. The scream pierced her reality and there was Michael above her, his eyes frightened, his mouth moving. His voice cut through. He was calling her name. Annabel's screaming and thrashing lasted as long as it took to register that there were no creatures swarming her.

She stopped abruptly, her heart hammering, her breath ragged. She looked around in bewilderment. Down at herself, then at the windows. There was nothing on her, and the windows were clear and bright.

"Are you alright?" said Michael.

She didn't know if she was or she wasn't. All she could say was, "I don't like this place."

Michael looked around the kitchen and gave a look that seemed to agree.

"I'm so tired of this," he said, finally.

"What?"

"Worrying about my sister. Do you want to wait in the van?"

Annabel thought about that then said, "No, I'll check the house with you, but keep hold of my hand."

He smiled. It was thin, but it was there, and he put his hand in hers and lifted her to her feet.

***

They went upstairs. Annabel didn't like the narrow stairway. It was enclosed, with an insipid light and bare walls. The two doors at the top of the stairs were both closed which made her feel even more closed in. There was no daylight. The hairs on her neck bristled as she walked up. Michael was ahead of her. Annabel felt like someone was about to grab her from behind.

At the top of the stairs, Michael opened the left hand door. Daylight spilled into stairway and Annabel was relived. Michael entered a bedroom. It was very untidy, unmade bed, dirty sheets, clothes all over the floor and, again, bare walls, covered in markings. There were pieces of torn wallpaper all over the carpet and a smell of damp and dried sick.

On seeing his sister's room, Michael became frantic. He started to shout her name, over and over. He ran from the bedroom, across the stairway, and burst into the back bedroom. Annabel thought she saw movement in the room when Michael entered but then couldn't be sure. Since entering the house, her sense of reality had been skewed. She'd only been in the house a short time and it had turned her inside out. The ladybirds had felt so real, the sense of dread was overwhelming, as was the sense that they were not alone. Every ounce of her being was screaming at her to GET OUT of the house, but Michael looked so distressed, she couldn't leave him. She wouldn't leave anyone alone in that house. The place was bad. Annabel had only ever been in one house that had had such an effect on her but this one was worse. Far worse.

Michael rushed to the window, peered down into the yard then went into the bathroom. Nothing. Nobody. He was still calling his sister's name and was becoming increasingly frightened. Annabel tried to make sense of her fear, attempting to understand its root cause. There were the markings—and the back bedroom was no different to the front, and the downstairs, bare, adorned with symbols and lettering—and there were the hallucinations but there was also the overwhelming feeling of wickedness about the house. It made her feel dizzy. If she didn't get out soon she knew she would start screaming and wasn't sure if she'd be able to stop.

Michael rushed from the room and ran back down the stairs. He didn't wait for Annabel and she had to run after him.

She nearly slipped on the stairs, but managed to right herself. She found Michael at the back door. He stepped out into the yard. He didn't see the black shape stood behind him, stood over him. Annabel only had a split second to register it before it was gone, but it had been there, of that much she was certain.

She stood in the kitchen while Michael shouted his sister's name across the backyards. She watched him through the window, saw him check out the outhouse, then she felt something behind her. Something on the stairs. That's when she started screaming.

Michael ran back into the kitchen and rushed to grab Annabel before she collapsed into hysteria.

"GET ME OUT OF HERE!" she screamed, and Michael pulled her across the kitchen floor and back through the front room. She never did look back to whatever was stood on the stairs.

Michael got her to the front door, pulled it open then led them out into the street. She stopped screaming then. She nestled her head into his chest and sobbed.

He took her to the van and opened the passenger door. He lifted her in and said, "I've got to go back inside."

Annabel shook her head violently. "Don't go back in there," she said. "That place is not right."

Michael deliberated. He looked tired.

Annabel said, "Let's just go to the gig. I need to be around people."

"It's my sister."

"I know, Michael. But she's not here, which means she's safe, away from that house."

"But what if she comes back?"

Annabel didn't say anything.

He shut the van door and she called for him, frantic.

Michael ran to the door but found it shut firm. He couldn't remember closing it when they came out. He fumbled about with his keys, found the one, slid it into the lock again, but this time it wouldn't turn. He tried and tried, getting more and more frantic. He started kicking and banging on the door, calling Heather's name, but the door wouldn't open.

***

Heather heard her brother shouting, but it was in a faraway place. She sat in the cellar, staring at the hole. Some part of her registered the banging on the door above, her name being called, but she couldn't move. Her eyes remained fixed on the hole.

Finally her brother went away, and the house fell silent again. And she waited. She waited for Rafferty to return.

PART FOUR
1976/2019

CHAPTER THIRTY-TWO

Poppy Elizabeth Lowes was born five weeks premature, on October 4th, 1976. The due date was November 7th. She was jaundice and frail and later developed septicaemia, which almost killed her. It was only by some miracle that she survived.

Now, having just turned forty-three, she looked strong and healthy, carrying with her the wisdom of age, of experience. Michael thought of her as his own daughter, and she, in turn, thought of him as a father.

He leaned back in his chair and watched the woman sat across from him. The daughter of his sister. The daughter of a man called Anthony Lowes, who died in a car crash, just like Michael's own parents did.

It had begun to rain, and it tapped against the window pane. Michael could see out to the fields, at the murky, grey cold. He looked back to his niece.

"We are a haunted species," he said. She looked at him. "Haunted by the past, that is. By our own pasts, our memories, the people we've lost. They are always with us…"

Poppy went to speak, then stopped, looked to the window, to the rain, then turned back to her uncle. "But what we're haunted by is something very different. And you know that."

"Look at the rain out there," he said. "The way the light comes in through the window.

The dust on the hearth. The piles of newspapers. The ticking of the clock. My old guitar over there in the corner. The smell of this old house...this old man..."

She watched him.

"These are ordinary, everyday things. Reality, you could say. But they are a veneer of reality. Most people only see these surface things, and I envy them. We have seen beyond this thin veneer and we can never go back. I wish I could have protected you from it...I tried, Poppy...I really tried..."

"I know."

"We are haunted by the ghosts of many," Michael said, softly. "A Cabal. They chose us. I don't know why. I think they've been with us....with our line...since your grandparents died in that car crash. I think that event opened some kind of door. In your mother, anyway. She became *susceptible*, as they say. And then when she moved onto Society Place...the door was kicked wide open."

CHAPTER THIRTY-THREE

Chloe found her husband in the Half Moon, sat in his usual spot at the end of the bar. He knew everyone in the pub, yet he drank alone. He was in every night after all, and at the weekend, afternoons and evenings. Chloe saw that Richard clocked her as soon as she walked in, but he offered no greeting. Instead he knocked his pint back and engaged the barman in ordering another. Chloe wasn't offered a drink.

She turned heads as she walked up to her husband. It made her sick to think of this man as her husband but there you go. Choices were made, paths were taken, and now…now she lived alone with an alcoholic husband, a missing child, and a ghost. It was no wonder she was following her husband into alcoholism.

"What do you want?" said Richard, supping his new pint.

"I want to know if you're ever going to come home?"

Chloe looked at him, then around the pub. She was the only female in the place. All the men looked the same, rigger boots, dirty clothes, ruddy noses, hard stares.

She turned back to her husband. "You do realise that our boy is missing, don't you?"

"Course I bleeding do. What the fuck are you going on about?"

"It's just you don't seem to care. It doesn't seem to have impacted your life one iota."

"I've been looking for him, haven't I?"

"You went out one night and ended up in here."

"Well...he's probably run away."

"And that doesn't concern you? He's nine years old, Rich, not nineteen. Have you thought to ask yourself why he might have run away from home?"

"Have you?"

Her expression darkened. "I know he didn't run away. He was taken."

"Taken?"

"Yes. He was taken by *them*."

"Now don't start on about that again. Especially not in 'ere. They'd think us mad, woman."

She looked around. "Do you think I give a fuck what these saddos think?"

"Don't come it in 'ere, Chloe. I'm warning ya."

"Look, our son has been taken by the things on our street."

"I don't have to listen to this."

"Richard. You know it to be true. Deep down, you know. I know you've seen things as well."

Her husband wouldn't meet her gaze.

"You know...don't you?" she said.

He took a long swallow of ale then placed the glass on the bar. Finally he looked at her. "Maybe I 'ave seen things. Maybe I've seen that little girl in our house. Maybe I've seen things when I've been out in the yard, down the jitty, up in the backs of people's houses. Maybe I've seen many of them watching me. Maybe I've seen things when I'm walking back from the pub—maybe I saw a hand coming up from the grate in that woman's cellar one night. But I don't know what you want me to do about it, Chloe?"

"Acknowledge it, Richard. That would be a start. Then we could work on where to look for our son."

They both fell silent. Chloe took a step closer to her husband and he looked at her. His eyes were teary and he wiped them with the back of his hand. For a moment, a brief moment, she glimpsed the man she married a decade before.

She rested a hand on the bar and found his hand. She didn't hold his hand, only touched it lightly, but it was enough. It was a connection. The most they'd had for a long time.

"I think he's under the house, Rich. Under the street. We have to go and get him."

Richard looked down at her hand, then back to his wife. He said, "I know."

***

Amar Singh wiped off the dog shit from his windows and then closed up. It was a little before ten, but he knew no one would be coming into the shop at this time. Not on a Tuesday night. He went out front to bring in the paper rack and that's when he saw Heather Lowes cresting the rise, walking in the middle of the road.

He called her name, but she didn't seem to hear him. She was heavily pregnant now and only seemed to be wearing a dressing gown. Amar checked the road for cars. There were none approaching, but still, one could be along any moment, and Mrs Lowes didn't seem to be aware of her surroundings. She looked out of it, vacant.

Amar ran over to her. She didn't notice him approach. The light of the city twinkled behind her. She looked lost.

"Heather!" he called as he got nearer. "Mrs Lowes!"

She finally noticed him and stopped walking. Amar reached her. She didn't look good. For one thing she looked cold, which wasn't surprising given the lack of clothes she had on, but more than that, she looked different, like there was nobody home. The spark in her eyes was gone.

She looked at Amar and spoke, softly. She said, "There are many things in my house."

Amar knew what she was talking about.

***

Candlestick Park tore into their last song of the set: Black Sabbath's *Paranoid*—a staple of their set lists and the one they usually ended on. The audiences at Talk of the Midlands always went crazy for it. The gig, their first in many weeks, had gone well, but Michael had simply been going through the motions. He had too much on his mind, too much worry clinging to him, to fully embrace the music. This was rare for Michael, although his loyalty to the band made sure he at least turned up to the gig. He thought playing might take his mind off the events at 2, Society Place. It didn't though. Usually the hit of his electric guitar was enough to blow away the world. Any problems or worries (or grief) he'd ever felt in his life, playing music would always funnel joy into him, even if it was only for the time spent actually in the song. The striking of a chord, that sound, that beautiful fury blasting back at him through his amplifier, was enough. It was a life preserver, a therapeutic wall of sound that would wrap around him, blocking out the darkness. But on that night in early October 1976, the music couldn't blow away Michael's worries, not even temporarily.

He messed up on the solo and Pete looked over at him, scowling. The audience didn't seem to notice, a line of long-hairs headbanging at the front of the stage.

The song (and set) came to its end and the audience cheered and stamped their feet and shouted for more but the band were done. They'd already played their encore and had pushed their time slot to its limits.

It was time to hit the bar.

Only, Michael never made it to the bar. As they walked off stage, Pete yanked him by the scruff of the neck and pushed him into a corner.

"What the fuck is wrong with you?" he shouted in Michael face.

Michael could see Bill and Paul stood behind Pete looking decidedly uncomfortable.

"Hey, Grant? What the fuck..."

"What?" Michael protested.

"You played shit. You've *been* playing shit for weeks. Since the recording session."

Michael noticed Bill and Paul slink off to the bar. Pete had his hand flat against Michael's chest, his face inches from his own.

"We're about to go into the studio again and you're fuckin' up. Isn't this what you want?"

Pete let the question hang.

Then, when no answer was forthcoming, he continued. "That girl is fuckin' your head up, mate. You're letting a split-arse mess with your head. This is what's real, mate. This is what we've been working for. Get your fuckin' head out your arse, Mike. You're not fucking this up for me, you 'ear?"

Then Annabel appeared at their side, shoving Pete away.

Things escalated very quickly after that.

It became a tussle, a lot of pulling and shoving. Michael later remarked on what a juvenile end it was to the band, to all that promise, all those dreams. It seemed to come from nowhere, Pete's anger that is, but deep down Michael knew it'd been building for a long time.

At one point Pete shoved Annabel and screamed at her to FUCK OFF and that was it. Michael went for him and fists were flown, things were said, and by the time Bill and Paul had raced over and pulled them apart, it was all over. Everything. And Michael knew it in an instant.

Pete's parting shot as Paul dragged him away was, "I hope you've got what you wanted."

They'd had bust-ups before, but this one felt different. This one felt like a deep scar.

Pete left shortly after that, leaving the rest of the band to pack up all the gear. But that was nothing new.

They still planned to go into the studio that weekend, as they were booked to do. The plan was to record an EP and attract some record company interest, and as they parted that night, that plan was still very much on the cards, despite what had happened. They loaded up the van from the side door of the club. Paul was saying that Pete will cool down and it'll all be alright, that kind of thing, but he didn't sound very convinced. Bill said very little.

Michael and Annabel got in the van and Michael fired up the engine. He heard Paul shout, "See you Saturday," and then Michael watched his bass player and his drummer walk off down the alleyway and back into the club. Something told him then that he would never play with them again.

He drove home.

CHAPTER THIRTY-FOUR

Amar Singh walked Heather back down the rise, leading her home. He'd taken her into his shop initially, calling his wife, Harsha, and covering Heather with a blanket. Amar fixed some tea while Harsha comforted her, but Heather was very quiet and unresponsive. Harsha kept asking if there was anyone they could call for her. They had a telephone, she said, and it would be no trouble, but Heather just shook her head and said there was no one she could call. Harsha had looked at Amar then, full of concern.

Heather stayed in the shop for about three quarters of an hour, Harsha holding her hand while she spoke soft, comforting words. Amar turned the main lights off, leaving half the shop in darkness; only a small light above the counter illuminated the area they were sat. After a time, Heather said she was fine and that she wanted to go home. Mr and Mrs Singh looked troubled by this change in her, but she must have convinced them because shortly after that Amar was walking her back down the rise.

Before she left, Harsha had told her to call on them any time she needed, and pressed the issue quite firmly. Heather said she would. Then, approaching her front door, Heather wished she had stayed with Harsha Singh. She wished she never had to go back into that house again.

Amar held her around the waist and guided her to her door.

She didn't want him to see inside her house, so she thanked him and rushed through the door. She heard him calling her name as the door slammed shut.

Inside, the nest of ghosts were waiting and Heather's first contraction started.

Five weeks before her due date.

CHAPTER THIRTY-FIVE

Michael and Annabel drove back to the flat in silence. He didn't even put on his 8-track. There was just the sound of the engine, and the lights of the city moving across their faces. Michael thought of his band, of his parents, of his sister. He thought about how strange Annabel had been after their visit to Heather's house. How it changed her.

She wanted to go to the gig, but once there she seemed to withdraw even further into herself. Now Michael was now sick with worry over his sister, and confused by Annabel's dark mood. He regretted going, for so many reasons, and later, when he realised that it was to be his last time performing on stage, the regret turned to hurt.

"I'm glad you came tonight," he said, trying to break the silence between them.

She looked at him. "Me too." She didn't mean that.

He looked at the side of her face. The lights of the city moving over her. She didn't look at him.

She said, "You're never going to make it."

"What?" He slowed down.

Finally she looked at him. "The music, I mean...you're never going to get to where you want to be."

He didn't say anything at first; he was too stunned. He turned down a side street and pulled over.

He left the engine ticking over. "Why would you say that?"

"Because it's true. I'm sorry. You are talented, but you don't really have what it takes."

Michael was shocked by how much this hurt. He would reflect later on, much later on, that it was perhaps the most hurtful thing that anybody had ever said to him, or ever would say to him.

"You're a marked man, Michael. But not by musical genius. No, you're marked in a very different way. I know things...I've always known things. In school I could tell which kids were in pain, who was being abused, which teachers had dark designs."

"What the hell are you talking about?"

"I'm saying I know all the bad things. Always have. I feel the weight of people, of their pain, their fear, their horror. I'm not for you Michael, yours is a different path."

"You breaking up with me?"

"Michael, you're not listening. I couldn't be with you even if I wanted to be."

He looked out the windscreen. An insipid yellow street light illuminated dark cars and house fronts.

"I don't understand."

She looked at him. "Your path is not mine to take. You will do a good thing. A very good thing but it will cost you."

She turned to open the van door.

"Wait! Where are you going?"

She stepped out of the van and turned to look at him. "I have my own path, Michael.

Take care of yourself. I will remember you fondly."

"Please...don't go. We can talk about this..."

"No Michael, you need to go. Your sister needs you."

CHAPTER THIRTY-SIX

Heather Lowes, once Heather Grant, lived until she was twenty-four years old. She was once a bright and happy child, from a loving family, but death had reared its head and dismantled her life piece by piece. Her parents had died in a car crash, late at night on a bypass not twenty miles from the stretch of road that would eventually kill her husband. She was an orphan at fourteen, a widow at twenty-four. Some lives are destined to be sad, full of pain and loss and horror. Heather Lowes, a sweet girl born to an unassuming family in the dry and barren East Midlands, was one such life. Hers was a brief spark, a flickering flame, a life with so much left undone. Yet, from her and Anthony Lowes' brief time on earth, they created a life. A gift. A girl.

***

On that final night on Earth, Heather found her house in a vortex of supernatural turmoil. The kitchen had been upturned. The cupboards were all open, the plates and crockery all over the floor. The table was upturned. The chairs stacked on one another. The house seemed to groan, the walls appeared to heave. Her front room had been the same. The television face down in the carpet, smashed to pieces. The settee was torn to shreds. She knew she should have got out of the house, but the contractions were too great, the pain flooding her in ever-increasing waves. Moreover, she knew that the things within the house would never let her go now. Instead she made for her bed.

But first, she had to get up the stairs.

***

Michael turned into Society Place and had to slam on the brakes. People all along the street were fleeing their houses. The lights inside all the houses were flickering. Michael could hear the banging and crashing coming from within the houses above the engine. People were screaming, shouting, running from their homes.

Michael abandoned his van in the middle of the road and jumped out.

He started to run.

***

The stairs were dark. Like a black void. A chamber from which there was no coming back from.

Heather stood at the foot of the stairs. Another contraction came and she doubled over, locking her teeth together and hissing in pain. Behind her the cupboard doors began to bang, open and shut, open and shut. The back door opened and Heather smelt the night. Rain was coming. She cried out and took the first step.

The bulb at the top of the stairway flickered. The presence floated up by the ceiling. It wasn't a fully formed entity, but a shape, a thin membrane over the fabric of reality. It lingered up there and Heather took another step, and then another. The house was rattling, noises, bangings, scrapings, all through the house.

Another contraction came and Heather screamed out. She held her belly and wailed. Her bedroom door looked a long, long way away.

***

Michael ran towards his sister's house. The only house whose door was firmly shut. Some residents fled the street altogether, others stopped and watched the paranormal activity within their homes, the flickering lights, the smashing of furniture, the nest of ghosts rattling their chains and moaning their moans.

Michael reaches his sister's house. Mrs Green was already banging on Heather's front door. He heard the noise coming from inside. Mrs Green looked stricken and moved back to allow Michael to try the door. He tried his key, but that didn't work, of course. Whatever was inside that house with his sister didn't want visitors.

"You have to help her," said Mrs Green, crying. "You have to get in there!"

Michael shouted his sister's name and smashed the weight of his body against the door.

***

There seemed to be more stairs. Many more. And they were steeper too. Heather crawled on her hands and knees, screaming in pain, in fear, in anger. The house raged around her. She knew the thing was floating above her. She felt long nails connect with her back.

Another contraction. She bit into the stair carpet, then carried on, upwards, forever upwards.

The door was now within touching distance.

The thing was at her neck, at her ear. She stopped moving.

She smelt its stench, rancid, vile. She gagged.

It spoke, its voice low, sounding very far away.

We follow you...we follow you and yours...

***

Michael banged on the door.

"Heather! Heather!"

A woman approached him. She was pretty, young, dark hair. She looked very distressed. A large man trailed behind her.

The woman said, "Hi, you must be Michael?"

"Yes."

"I'm Chloe. I'm a friend of your sister's."

"Have you seen her?"

"No. She's in the house. My son's in there too...in the hole."

***

Heather cried out as she stood and took the last remaining steps to the bedroom door. Before she reached the handle, the door opened.

***

Michael and the woman's husband took it in turns to bash all their weight against the front door.

***

Heather entered the bedroom. The room was bright, but not illuminated by electricity, this was an unnatural light, an unearthly light, bright and white and scorching to the eye. She narrowed her eyes and reached for the bed.

She never made it.

A huge contraction dropped her to her knees and she fell face first on the edge of the bed.

The noise in the house was still piercing.

The baby was coming. Her baby. Heather screamed and screamed and screamed.

***

In the cellar a boy stood. He didn't know his name, who he was, how he got there. His clothes were rags. His skin was bruised, battered, lacerated.

He looked at the hole and then turned his back on it.

***

Heather Lowes started to push the baby that had grown inside her, out. The baby that Anthony Lowes, her dead husband, had given her.

We follow you and yours.

She felt blood run down her legs. She kept her eyes closed to the supernatural light burning in her room. So bright it seemed to hum. There were things in the light, she knew that, but she didn't look at them. She could sense them, feel them, watching her.

She felt the baby's head crowning. The spirits raged, cried out, let loose terrible moans and howls.

This noise was then chimed with the crying of a baby as it slipped from the vagina and was caught by her mother's hand.

***

The door gave. The lock smashed, the door flung inwards.

***

The boy ascended the stairs. To the light.

***

Heather opened her eyes and looked at the baby in her arms. The crying baby. Her daughter. Alive, very alive. Heather felt the blood rushing out of her and onto the floor. Her head spun.

Her little girl looked at her and stopped crying. The light dimmed a little. The noise, the fucking noise, finally gave. The things in the house, behind the veil of reality, moved away.

Heather let loose tears and stroked her daughter's face.

Behind her the boy stood watching.

There was blood all over the floor.

Before she died, Heather smiled and felt a surge, a beautiful heart-searing surge of love for the girl in her arms.

***

Michael was the first in. He raced through the house, followed by Chloe and her husband. Everything was upturned but Michael hardly noticed.

He raced through the front room, through the kitchen, and up the stairs.

What he found in the bedroom brought him to his knees.

His sister was dead, against the bed, splayed in a pool of her own blood.

There was a young boy. The boy Michael had seen out on the street. The boy whose parents were coming up the stairs behind him.

The boy was stood holding a baby. A bloody crying baby.

Michael heard the woman call her son's name on seeing him but Michael didn't move. He watched as the mother and father crowded the boy. The father took the baby from the boy allowing the mother to hold him, hug him, love him.

The father brought the baby to Michael and placed it in his hands then the father went away to his son.

Michael looked at the body of his sister. A woman. A mother, who brought this little girl into the world.

Michael looked at the little girl and the little girl looked at him.

He said, "Poppy," and stroked her head.

CHAPTER THIRTY-SEVEN

Forty-three years later, Michael watched Poppy Lowes drive away from him for the last time and went inside to sit watching the fire. He picked up his old acoustic guitar and idly strummed. He'd bought it brand new in 1973 and it'd cost him an arm and a leg back then, although he could no longer remembered the exact price. It was a Martin and had always had a beautiful tone to it, even now, all these years later. It was faded and worn, scratched and chipped here and there, but it still sang. He had composed *Hey Girl* on it back in 1975, along with a few other originals he'd written for Candlestick Park, and he'd continued to write songs on it down the years. Songs no one ever heard. The guitar had seen him through so much, and he felt comfort playing it. As he did now, gentling picking out notes and chord progressions as he listened to the pop and snap of the wood being eaten by the fire.

From his position in his chair by the fire, he could see out to the field at the back of his house. Churned earth and dull sky. He allowed his thoughts to drift, to his parents, the car crash, his band, what they could have been, and to his sister, Heather. His father had told him to look after her, but he could not. She was beyond his help, so he did the next best thing he could, he gave his life to bringing up Heather Lowes's daughter. The daughter that was now a woman, with a family of her own, who lived far across the Atlantic Ocean, far away from England, from Derby. From Society Place.

He thought of Poppy as a baby, how sick she'd been, how he didn't think she'd ever pull through, and then, just like that, her blood started pumping again and she sprung to life. He thought of the house they lived in during the eighties, a small semi in Belper, a good twenty miles outside of Derby. Poppy had gone to school there, they'd had Christmases and Bonfire nights and long summers together. It was always just him and her. They had their life together, and although at times it was bloody hard, they were happy—Michael was happy.

He continued to work as a painter and decorator, and they lived a modest life. Poppy had called him daddy when she was little, then when she got a little older, just after she left school, she tried calling him Dad, but by then it didn't feel right to either of them. Yet it hurt his heart when she took to just calling him Michael.

When she was twenty-four she went on holiday to America, and while out there she met Martin, and that was that. She left England, and Michael, a year later.

For the first few years, Poppy and Martin flew over to see him quite regularly, at least twice a year, then as the years went on, and they had Heather, it became less and less. But now she was back, all alone, and not a word to him that she was even coming. It concerned him greatly. Even after their conversation, he still wasn't sure why she was here. It was good see her. Michael didn't let on just how good it was to see her, but still, her presence troubled him greatly. In America she was safe, whereas here, she was wide open to whatever still lingered beyond the fringes of human comprehension. Plus, she was susceptible to the channelling. Just like her mother was. They were transistor radios picking up frequencies beyond this world. They were tuned into the dead, and the dead seemed to know this. *They* were drawn to Poppy, just as they were to Heather.

Michael began to play *Hey Girl*, slowing the song's tempo right down, picking at the chords, and began to sing in low range. He never took his eyes off the field, and the black shape wavering in the wind. It was always out there. Watching him. Waiting for him.

He stopped playing and began to cry. He knew he wouldn't see Poppy again, as surely as he knew she would go to Society Place. He knew it pulled at her. It always had.

"I'll just sit here," he said to the shape out in the field. "I couldn't look after either of them." He wiped away the tears with the backs of his hands. "But you knew that, didn't you..." He rested the guitar up against the wall. The shape shifted in the wind.

"So I'll just sit here, and wait."

The breeze carried the shape down the field, closer to his house.

"I'll sit here and wait," he said a final time. He closed his eyes.

"I know you won't be long."

CHAPTER THIRTY-EIGHT

Rafferty Gilroy knew Poppy would return. He sat in his chair, in the darkness, waiting for her. He already had his tool bag packed and ready to go. The house was silent, save for the ticking of his clock. The television was black, and from the fading light filtering in from the kitchen, he could see his reflection. Or at least, his shape, sat there, motionless.

He thought of that row of houses stood about six miles from where he now sat. How they were empty, boarded up, but he could still feel their presence. He had always been able to feel them, ever since his time down there, beneath the floorboards, in the earth, with the nest, clawing and poking and jeering at his terror. They were shifting shapes, sometimes whole, sometimes faint, but always moving, merging into one another, bugling, pulsing, pressing their dead forms upon him. Their fat fingers probed his mouth as he screamed, they pulled at his hair, his arms, his legs. No part of him wasn't molested by them. Down there, in the dark, beneath the place he slept.

They didn't penetrate him but they certainly had their way with him. Their texture was rubbery and every touch, every poke and prod, took away more and more of the light inside him, until, after a while, he was no longer screaming, just letting their formless, shifting shapes to smother him.

The Once-Man watched from the mouth of the tunnel, and the other one: the ancient being that lived in Heather Lowes' house. Rafferty had caught their eyes and saw there was nothing human about them. No goodness, no light. They were dark beings, ancient and malevolent. Rafferty had the sense they were envious of his life, his light, and they wanted to take it, toy with it, corrupt it and watch the aftermath of such a destruction of spirit.

And here he was, after all these years, still corrupted, still destroyed. How they must laugh. They took away all he would have ever been, all he could have ever had, because they could, and to them, it was amusing. A game.

Heather Lowes, Rafferty believed, was different. She was a channel. Her life, her grief, perhaps even her pregnancy, gave them energy. It riled them up, like a predator to the smell of blood. She got them excited. Society Place had always been a haunted place, but after she arrived, the ghosts became increasingly hostile; accumulating in the night Poppy Lowes was born.

In 1993, Rafferty was approached by a bloke in a pub. The early nineties were the tail end of his drinking and drugging days but it wouldn't be 1995 until he was fully clean, only to lapse briefly again at the turn of the century. Still in '93 if someone offered to buy him a drink, he'd take it. So they got talking in a pub called The Neptune on the edge of town. The bloke was older than Raff by about ten years, perhaps more, and was certainly not from Derby. He was posh, and sounded it. Wore a smart suit, shiny shoes, and was clean shaven, save for a thin moustache. From around Raff's way, he was not.

He never got the man's name—Raff was five pints deep and it was only half one in the afternoon—but it quickly became apparent that this guy knew about Society Place, and about its strange history. He started to ask Raff all sorts of questions—*how long did you live there? How old were you when you moved away? Did you know a woman called Heather Lowes?* and so forth.

"You a journalist?" Raff had asked him. He'd had one or two journos sniffing around the story over the years, and one or two nut jobs—psychic investigators and all that bollocks—and he'd seen them all off. Yet, he indulged this chancer, at least for a little while.

"I'm a writer," he'd said. "Fiction mostly, but I have written the odd non-fiction book. I tend to lean towards the supernatural, the uncanny. I think the story of Society Place could be a bestseller. I can't believe no one has done it already, but perhaps it's because there is such little information, and well..."

"Well what?"

"Well, no one is talking. And I mean no one. But this event, this place, appears to have been a massive channel for the paranormal. Perhaps larger than the stories of Borley, the Enfield Poltergeist...maybe even Amityville."

"It's all bollocks," said Raff.

The bloke looked at him. "Really?"

"Yeah. You telling me you believe all that shit?"

The guy looked devastated. "Well, I—"

"Come on, man. It's kids stuff. I mean look around you. There's nothing more than meets the eye. People 'round here have got fuck all. We work, we come down the boozer, that's it. That's the fucking reality of it."

"But..."

"But what, man?"

"But you are Rafferty Gilroy aren't you?"

"Yeah."

"Well...Shaw told me you went down there."

Raff fell silent. He took a long drink, finishing the glass, then asked to the barman for another. Finally he turned back to the writer.

"You spoke to Shaw?"

"Yes, just before he died."

"Shaw's dead? Well, good riddance."

"Shaw died in that house."

"He went back there?"

"After they condemned the street, he broke back into number 2, and starved himself to death. I guess he just wanted to be with them."

"How do you know all this?" asked Raff, not wanting to know the answer.

"Because I watched him die, and I saw something take his body down into the cellar."

***

There was a knock on the door and Rafferty was dragged back to the present. He grabbed his tool bag and got up. He went out of the room and into the hallway. He could make out the silhouette of Poppy Lowes through the glass panels. He opened the door.

She looked at him. "You ready?"

"Yes," he said, and closed the door behind him.

CHAPTER THIRTY-NINE

The imposing Victorian structure of St Chad's Infant School was torn down in 2006, and was left as a patch of waste ground. With the school gone, the skyline lay open, revealing the twinkling lights of the city beyond. There was still a little light left in the western sky, but night was coming on fast and insipid yellow street lamps lit rows and rows of brick terraces all down the rise. The only street unlit was Society Place. A black strip on the panorama.

A great many windows were boarded up here and there, but most of the houses were still occupied on the rise. Doors were all shut, curtains were all drawn. Leaves scattered along pavements, a fox sniffed around the waste ground.

Poppy pulled the car up at the top of the rise, and they sat looking out across the waste ground to the right, and the row of terraces on the left. The coming dark brought forth more illumination from the city that lay sprawled out beyond this patch of ignored land. Poppy turned off the engine, but neither one of them moved.

Raff said, "I haven't been here for a long, long time."

Poppy remained silent. A plane far off to the west crossed the night sky, its lights flashing. "My school was here," continued Raff.

"When was it pulled down?"

"I don't know, ten years or more, maybe. I remember reading about it in the paper."

"You know, Normanton was once a Viking settlement," said Poppy.

"Really?"

"Yeah. It used to be called Normanestune, which apparently means Norseman's Settlement. It's mentioned in the Domesday Book."

Raff looked at her and she smiled.

"I hit Wikipedia on the flight over."

"I see," he said. "Sounds like a trope."

"What do you mean?"

"Well, haunted street built on an ancient settlement. More than likely this rise is one giant burial ground, just to round out the perfect ghostly back story."

She laughed, but there was no humour in it. "Hey, every town and city is built on some ancient settlement. Certainly in this creaky old country."

"True enough," he said.

The plane was now in the east, winking out from view.

Poppy said, "You really not been here since...well, since back then?"

"No, I think I came back one night in the late eighties or early nineties when I was out my face. I threw a few bottles at my old house and started raging. People still lived in them houses then and they called the police. Slept the night off in a cell and ended up in court. Ended up paying for damages."

"And that's the only time?"

"Yes. Me mum had just died, and well..."

"I'm sorry."

Raff nodded. "It was a long time ago."

"It was and it wasn't, right?"

"Yes," he said. "It was and it wasn't. Time is fucking weird."

They fell silent.

A car came up the rise, momentarily blinding them. They both ducked down until it had passed.

"Shit," said Poppy.

"Don't worry," said Raff. "Tomorrow you'll be on a plane back to America."

"And what about you?"

He didn't say anything.

They both looked at the dark strip of houses halfway down the rise. They could make out the rooftops, black against the city behind.

"Why was the street condemned?" asked Poppy. "I couldn't find any information about it online."

"The official word was that it was subsidence that had made all the structures unsafe. That might have been true. They are old Victorian terraces, built on a steep rise, but that was only part of the story. In truth, after the eighties, no one would buy a house on that street. There were just too many stories."

"Everyone knows about this place?"

Raff nodded. "It's like an open secret. Everyone around here knows something about what went on. I heard kids dare each other to run down it at night. Knock on a door and scarper."

"It's become an urban legend."

"I guess it has, yes. The council planned to pull it down and there was talk of doing it at the same time they did the school, but for some reason they never did. They've just left it to rot, but I guess they've left this entire area to rot."

"There are still people living in Corporation Street and...what's the other adjacent street?"

"Silver Hill Road. Yes, the houses on those streets are still occupied."

"So there's just this row of abandoned terraces sat crumbling away, surrounded by this community?"

"Yes. Like I said, Society Place is the black secret. Every town has a place like this; some are just more known or visible than others."

They fell silent again. Another plane crossed the night sky.

"Shall we do this then?" Poppy said.

"Yes," said Raff, and they got out of the car.

CHAPTER FORTY

"Houses have walls," said Shaw. "Bricks and mortar. They are built by hand, human hands, from the ground up. From foundations dug deep into earth."

Shaw's rotting bones lay on a dirty mattress on a hardwood floor.

"Windows let the light in. Roof trusses rest above us. Slates darken in the rain."

The writer watched from a corner in the room. The place smelt of decaying flesh and dried shit.

"Inside, bathrooms are fitted. Electricity is wired down walls and beneath floorboards. Beds are made. Ovens fill kitchens with aromas. Babies are born."

Shaw already looked like a spectre, a once-man, whose life had been nothing but a pursuit for death. For some kind of higher understanding of the universe.

"People grow. They weather storms, and laugh with joy, and cry into the night. There are Christmases and summers and autumn leaves that pile up in gardens. Doorsteps are swept. Curtains are drawn. People move in, people move away. Some feel trapped, others feel sanctuary. Some die."

The writer looked at the bag of bones laid on the mattress. Thin and worn curtains shaded the room but light edged its way in. It struck the writer how well Shaw still spoke. He didn't look like he'd be able to raise an arm, yet his voice, although hoarse, was still clear and articulate.

"They wallpaper and paint, fix doors and replace windows. They strip away the lingering scent of others and turn the bricks and mortar into a home—and the cycle goes on."

The writer remained in the corner, not wanting to get any closer to the thing on the bed.

"People live. People die. They love, they despair. Sometimes bad things happen. Sometimes there is beautiful tenderness. Every aspect of the human condition plays out. We are bled into the walls."

Shaw coughed and tongued his broken lips.

"And houses can stand for generations. Some cross into new centuries. Sometimes they are a home, other times, nothing but a shell."

Shaw looked at the writer.

"Yes, houses have walls. And they soak all of us up. Every last drop."

His eyes glassed over and the writer thought he was dead but then Shaw coughed again. A dry, guttural cough. A death rattle.

"They soak us up, and the things that move beside us cling to the bricks and mortar, feasting on the pain and laughter and sadness and wastes of life that seep into the walls. They drink us up. It keeps them here."

The writer heard someone out on the stairway and backed evermore into the corner.

"This was the woman's room. She gave birth in here, and then died. Think of all that energy seeping into this place. The two major events of life, birth and death, in a single moment."

Shaw turned his head and looked at the writer.

"My friends below feasted on it, and are thirsty for more."

The writer felt the presence out on the stairway.

"They are always thirsty."

The door began to push inwards.

"I have haunted this place for many years. This house...there is something about this house."

The writer looked again at the door and it was open. The stairway was dark.

"I watched that woman. I knew her grief. My friends fed off its black emanations. A grief like tar. Thick and congealed. And these walls drank it in. Swam in it. It was a feast of delights."

The writer finally spoke. "Your friends are here."

"I know," said Shaw. "They are always here. And now I will be with them. Forever."

"Are you not frightened?"

Shaw looked at him. "What is there to be frightened of? I will spend eternity feasting on the delights of human pain. What a glorious substance it is."

"Did your life have any meaning?" asked the writer. Something unseen entered the room.

Shaw looked at him, and then at the thing that had entered. "I was just passing through," he said then he closed his eyes.

The writer watched his final breath leave his body, and then Shaw was dragged from the mattress, across the floor and out onto the stairway. The writer remained stood in the corner, listening to the lifeless body thud down the stairs. Then there was movement in the kitchen below, and finally more hollow thuds as the body was cast down into the cellar. Then all was silent.

The writer gripped his right hand to stop it from shaking. It took him a long time to be able to walk to the stairway and descend down into the house and find his way out again.

***

The writer killed himself three days after talking to Rafferty Gilroy in a pub called The Neptune.

His book died with him.

CHAPTER FORTY-ONE

Poppy Lowes stood in the room she was born in. She had not been in the house since she was taken from it in the moments after her birth, so none of it was recognisable to her. It was to Rafferty Gilroy though. Stood beside Poppy, both stood with slicing torchlight in hand, Rafferty seemed short of breathe. Poppy could sense his unease.

"You okay?" she asked him.

He simply nodded, but she knew he was far from okay. He was terrified.

They had broken in through the back way. Raff had led her down a jitty (she had to be reminded of what this regional word meant: she called it an alleyway) and passed the roots and stump of an old tree. The back gate was hanging off its hinges, so they had easy access to the back yard. Their torches probed the dark and Poppy got her first look at the house she was born in. All the windows were boarded up, as was the back door.

To the left of the yard were the rotted remains of an outhouse. Poppy shone the torch in and screwed up her face at the sight of the filthy toilet piled up with rubbish and dead leaves and old newspapers. The yard was cracked and broken, tall weeds bursting forth. The fence had fallen into next door's yard, and rubbish lay here and there.

Rafferty dropped his tool bag and pulled out a cordless drill and quickly went about unscrewing the boarding from the door. That done, he lay the board down onto the fallen fence, and then turned his attention to the back door. The glass panelling was already smashed in, and the door itself was thin and rotten. One firm kick at the handle was enough to smash it open.

Poppy knew that before they did anything, she wanted to see the bedroom where she was born. Rafferty was reluctant to indulge in this, but had finally agreed, so long as they were quick. The kitchen smelt damp and a little like rotten eggs. Old units had fallen in on themselves and now just looked like broken piles of wood. The place was pitch-black and their torchlight cut through in long slices, illuminating only what was directly in its line of sight.

Poppy shone the light on the dark opening of the stairway and crossed the kitchen slowly and carefully. Rafferty followed.

At the mouth of the stairs, Poppy directed her light upwards, illuminating the narrow passageway and revealing two closed doors set either side of a small landing. The stairs themselves were fragile and had to be taken carefully. At the top of the stairs Poppy instinctively knew that the front bedroom was her mother's and the room she was born in. Rafferty confirmed this as she pushed the door inwards and asked, "This it?"

And now here they were in a fusty, dirty room, with a boarded up window, with nothing but a blackened and skeletal mattress in one corner, its rusty and wiry springs exposed.

"I feel no connect to the place," she said.

"Why should you?" said Raff. "The place is just a rotten shell. Any light here is long gone."

Poppy thought on this for a moment, then said: "What was she like?"

Raff looked at her, half-illuminated behind her beam of light. "She was a lovely woman," he said. "She was sad, but kind. You were inside her when I knew her, and she was always holding her belly...holding you. Protecting you."

Poppy choked back tears. "Michael told me what she did to bring me into the world. How she fought off...*them*."

Raff took a step closer to her. "I saw her look into your eyes in the moments after your birth. She was filled with love for you before she died."

Poppy allowed the tears to fall. "She was all alone here," she said. "All alone with the dead."

"You said your daughter has seen your mother?"

"Yes."

"Well, don't you see what that means?"

"No."

"It means she got out of here. She wasn't dragged down into the nest. Her spirit flew, Poppy. Flew to you and your family." Raff put a hand on her shoulder and gently squeezed.

She looked at him. "Her family," she said.

"Yes."

Raff let her cry it out a moment longer, then said, "Come on, we better do this, before *they* stir."

CHAPTER FORTY-TWO

Poppy stood at the top of the landing and shone her torch down the stairs, the light a sharp line against the utter blackness. She did not want to go down there. She did not like the stairway. Raff stood at her mother's old bedroom door and was shaking again. She knew this because his light would not hold true. She looked at him and he tried to smile. It was meant to be reassuring but just came off as weak and pitiful. She took a step down and she immediately sensed something at the bottom of the stairs.

"Oh God," she said. The blackness seemed to shift at the knife edges of her light.

"You can do this, Poppy," Raff said, but his voice was unsteady.

She closed her eyes and took another step. It creaked beneath her, sounding very loud to her ears.

Another step. Something moved through her light beam. It was faint, but something did move at the bottom of the stairs.

"I can't do this," she said.

"We have to," replied Raff.

Another step. She felt the thing rush up to meet her and she froze. It remained at the outer dark. She moved the torchlight, but the thing shifted again. Now she was shaking. Her light thrown around the dark but it never found the thing on the stairs. Instead, the thing on the stairs found her.

It came to her ear and she felt its coldness, its deadness, and she smelt its stink. Then *it* whispered, very faint, seemingly very far away, and yet, as intimate as a lover at her neck.

We've waited for you.

She put her hand to her mouth, holding back the scream in her throat.

Come.

"Poppy?" said Raff behind her. "Are you alright?"

She had her hand clasped tight to her face, her eyes watering and bulging with a terror beyond rational thought.

"Poppy..."

Come down with us.

"Poppy..."

The nest waits.

She closed her eyes and thought of her mother. Of the strength she must have had to survive long enough to bring her into the world.

"Fuck you," she said to things within those dark walls. She raced off down the stairs.

Raff followed after her.

She crossed the kitchen to the back door and Raff felt sure she was fleeing, but then she returned with his tool bag.

She looked at him across the dark and ruined kitchen, their torch lights crossing at the centre of the room, and she said, "Let's burn this fucking place to the ground."

***

They started in the cellar. Raff had already pre-soaked several bundles of paper and rags and these he threw deep into the hole then he made sure to douse the cellar with petrol. That done, he spat into the hole.

They had a can each and busied themselves dousing the entire downstairs. Raff made a trail up the cellar stairs and made short work of the front room. Poppy did the kitchen. There was enough paper and rubbish scattered about, not to mention the wooden kitchen units, along with a pile of old curtains in the front room, that any chance of the fire not catching was very slim.

Her canister almost empty, Poppy splashed her dregs up the stairs then threw the canister itself up to the landing where it came to rest with a hollow thud.

After this they stood in the kitchen, both of them panting, listening to the house.

They listened until they heard movement in the cellar below, then Poppy lit the match and they fled number 2, Society Place.

CHAPTER FORTY-THREE

Michael stepped out of number 2, Society Place. The baby in his arms.

There were blue lights from the ambulance and police cars. Radio voices, people rushing in and out of Heather's house, and then there were the residents of Society Place, all looking to Michael and the baby he carried.

Mrs Green was the first to step forward. She came to Michael with a fragile look of hope, but when he simply shook his head, the old woman cried out and dropped to her knees. Chloe caught her and held onto her. Her son, Rafferty, looked at Michael, and Michael didn't like those dead, haunted eyes, and he turned away from him.

He looked at the baby in his arms, naked still, caked in blood, and he felt tears run down his face.

The baby opened her eyes and looked at him, and in those eyes he saw his sister, and his mother.

There is a line of ghosts within us all, he thought.

CHAPTER FORTY-FOUR

They lit the night with flames. They went to the top of the rise and watched the strip of fire amongst the rows and rows of brick houses. From their vantage point, they could see the blue lights flashing out in the city, approaching fast. The stars glistened overhead and Poppy cast her eyes from the flames engulfing Society Place and looked to the night sky.

"All that universe," she said, "all that infinite space. A tiny street in such vastness, and my mother and I ended up there."

Rafferty watched the fire, the sirens close enough to hear now.

"Some are born to sweet delight," he said. "Some are born to endless night."

The wind picked up and scattered leaves down the road.

EPILOGUE – BEFORE

The woman who showed them around had Farrah Fawcett hair. Anthony held Heather's hand as they moved from the front room and into the kitchen. The Farrah Fawcett estate agent gave them the big sell but Heather wasn't really feeling an attachment to the house. Houses are like that, they have feelings to them. You can sense their nature.

The estate agent showed them around the kitchen. It was grimy, looked old, unloved. In fact, the house looked like it had never been loved.

While they were stood in the kitchen, Heather looked to the dark stairway that led off the kitchen. Something about it unnerved her.

She turned her back to it and looked at her husband. At the side of his face. She had Wings' *Silly Love Songs* going around her head.

The estate agent took them upstairs. Heather didn't like the stairway.

They looked at both bedrooms, and the basic bathroom in the back room. Heather noticed a large tree hanging over all the backyards. She liked the tree.

They all went back downstairs to the kitchen, the heart of any house.

The estate agent talked details. The price was right, certainly for them, and Anthony seemed excited about the place.

She turned her back on the stairway.

She looked at the side of his face again and knew that they would buy the house.

She found his hand and imagined their future together.

BIOGRAPHY

Andrew David Barker is an author and filmmaker. Born in Derby in 1975, his books include *The Electric*, *Dead Leaves*, and the children's story, *The Winterman*. As a filmmaker he is the writer and director of the micro-budget post-apocalyptic feature *A Reckoning* and several award-winning short films. He lives in Warwickshire with his wife and daughters, trying to be a grown up.

Also By Andrew David Barker

The Electric

Dead Leaves

For Children

The Winterman

Collections

Winter Freits

(Black Shuck Shadows 9)

ADRIAN BALDWIN (COVER ARTIST)

Adrian is a Mancunian now living and working in Wales. Back in the 1990s, he wrote for various TV shows/personalities: Smith & Jones, Clive Anderson, Brian Conley, Paul McKenna, Hale & Pace, Rory Bremner (and a few others). Wooo, get him! Since then, he has written three screenplays—one of which received generous financial backing from the Film Agency for Wales. Then along came the global recession which kicked the UK Film industry in the nuts. What a bummer! Not to be outdone, he turned to novel writing—which had always been his real dream—and, in particular, a genre he feels is often overlooked; a genre he has always been a fan of: Dark Comedy (sometimes referred to as Horror's weird cousin). *Barnacle Brat* (a dark comedy for grown-ups), his first novel won Indie Novel of the Year 2016 award; his second novel *Stanley Mccloud Must Die!* (more dark comedy for grown-ups) published in 2016 and his third: *The Snowman And The Scarecrow* (another dark comedy for grown-ups) published in 2018. Adrian Baldwin has also written and published a number of dark comedy short stories. He designs book covers too—not just for his own books but for a growing number of publishers. For more information on the award-winning author, check out:
https://adrianbaldwin.info/

DEMAIN PUBLISHING

To keep up to-date on all news DEMAIN (including future submission calls and releases) you can follow us in a number of ways:

BLOG:
www.demainpublishingblog.weebly.com

TWITTER:
@DemainPubUk

FACEBOOK PAGE:
Demain Publishing

INSTAGRAM:
demainpublishing

Printed in Great Britain
by Amazon